The Visitor - Known and Unknown

Anni's Diary

The Visitor - Known and Unknown

Anni's Diary

by

Zoltan Karpathy

Copyright © 1997 by Zoltan Karpathy

All rights reserved. No part of this book may be reproduced, stored in a retrieval system, or transmitted by any means, electronic, mechanical, photocopying, recording, or otherwise, without written permission from the author.

ISBN: 1-58721-067-3

Copyrighted at the Library of Congress

1stBooks – rev. 03/01/2000

"About the Book"

A new novel; based on actual happenings, takes the reader from Europe to both coasts of the United States, where the second and third generation of women endure violence, rape, murder, and mis-justice of the system, that entails two trials.

The thrill and mystery fills every page, and comes to a surprising climax.

A well written, polished first novel.

Dedication

I dedicate my book to the memory of Anni Thompson and Helen Richter, and all the Anni Thompson's and Helen Richter's who are, or will be, the victims of similar crimes. Therefore, this dedication is also meant to be for the thirty percent of our country's female population whom, by the age of 30, have been affected by the crime that my story is based on.

Zoltan Karpathy

Preface

Perhaps the ultimate crime that my book deals with, is an all-consuming betrayal, against the human soul, body, and dignity.

As I delved further into the story, I came to the conclusion, that the crime has also robbed the freedom of the affected parties, and left a black mark on our justice system.

I am a European born male, and had my formal education from Gymnasium, and some college completed in Budapest.

I've lived in numerous countries in western Europe, and speak four languages.

In the late 1950's when I emigrated to the U.S.A., the different culture, law, and tolerance, awoke my curiosity to draw a parallel, between U.S.A. and the European civilization, as an all-inclusive history for both.

After forty years living in the U.S.A., and observing the deterioration of our justice system, my harsh decision of today's "drive-by justice system" is well founded, not singularly by me, but also by the echo of the consensus, of the overwhelming decent citizens of our country.

The indictment that my book partly concerns itself with, is a two-fold tragedy: namely education, and respect.

The staggering numbers relating to the crime, that is so often committed in our country, is incomparable to any other.

If we politicize every issue in our country, including criminality, and then arrogantly bring the verdict: that it must be working, since we are still here, and function as a nation, then we also must accept the fact, that a sewer tank does also operate under certain conditions: however, it must be cleaned out at times. It should be an important anomaly in the policy of our so-called system, and the essence of common-sense.

Our elected or appointed astute leaders, should adhere and practice the process, since we the public elected them to their positions, to do it, and not to misuse the trust, that we have invested in them, at the voting booths.

Listening to the echo of our nation, there is no doubt, that we are on the fast track of moral decline. The tolerance that we grant, for promiscuity to the most powerful, all the way to the urban teenager, overshoots the politically correct, sexual freedom excuse, and only mimics, Sodom and Gomorra, of biblical times, and more recently the decline and the destruction of the Roman Empire.

I am a firm believer, that life is a classroom, where history, and all lessons are learned.

If we would follow the right path, and put politics aside: the fungus could be cured.

If we would look to other nation's methods and crime rates: we could adopt their's, and giving up our misconstrued pride, would lower the crime rate.

Expectations in our country, became a political football, and not practiced on the field of life.

The slap on the wrist, became a common practice in our justice system, and no wonder: there are too many criminals in our country, for the law to deal with.

Most every nation is born of violence, but after some two hundred and twenty years, we should have learned how to educate, to minimize the effect on society, to the point of being manageable.

The true fact is: that as far as an educated society, we are out of hand.

I have raised the question in my mind, countless times, if not for economical reasons, but for the more important character, and moral one: the rest of the civilized world, laughs at us ..... or feels sad or sorry for us?

Either way, it is a sorry, but true indictment, on this otherwise great nation, that I am a part of, and try to be a doctor to it, partially by writing this book.

When healthy and well practiced traditions are put in limbo, in any society, as it's in our country: we should not be surprised of the ugly outcome, that we are presently faced with.

If we combine the aforementioned, with inadequate, or at best mediocre education: the catastrophe as history proved it, is always doom.

This book deals with one aspect of the many crimes, but also encompasses the dirty ingredients of others, that contributed to its history.

I felt, that this book had to be written, not just for the mere fact, that it is based on true happenings, but also for all of us, to look into the mirror of our conscience, and guilt, and wonder why we don't change our attitude, toward education, moral, tradition, and decency: that are the glue, to any healthy, and successful surviving society.

Without the moral fiber, no nation can weave the shroud, that will protect it, against the wrong directional progress, and the maggots that could consume it, to the point of decay.

My Villains in this book have used the system. My Heroines and Heroes have suffered under it, and the Administrators shamefully tolerated it.

There is a bigger lesson learned, as we read through the pages of this book, and the passion of its creator, cuts through all boundaries, whether pro or con: to give you the opportunity, to sit on the jury of conscience. But remember, the only verdict of your's should be: change.

This, our great nation, has survived countless calamities, and so the advice of this writer, is very simple. As we travel on this so far unsecured road, and come to a fork, let us not choose the Latin route (demise of Roman Empire) but the one, that will heal this nation: better education and respect.

I have read and studied Anni's "Diary."

I, as the writer, not only knew the people that were involved in this book, but was also detailed familiar with their life's history, and not arrogantly, but necessarily, became the narrator of it.

During my life time, I was involved in the entertainment field, real estate, and the owner and operator, of three restaurants, and cocktail lounges.

My extended world travel, speaking four languages, and the aforementioned businesses, brought me in close contact with numerous people, on various levels.

The experiences that I've made, and the lessons I've learned are an important effigies incorporated in the following pages.

As Mohammed said fifteen hundred years ago "Don't tell me how smart you are, but how much have you traveled."

<u>Introduction</u>

The most unbiased judgment comes from people who are not, or have never been affected by the conflict.

The question is: Should judgment be rendered on merit or following the book of law disregarding innocence or guilt.

We are still a laboratory of democracy and not a fully-matured nation. Therefore, some judgments are handed down that are contrary to all common sense.

Most of the laws are written to protect the innocent and punish the perpetrator. Unfortunately, some laws punish the innocent and protect the perpetrator.

The end of the United States is not Key West but the judicial system and the attitude of the people. I do not declare myself to be a drum major for justice, but after forty years of careful study and observation, I've come to the conclusion that justice in our country is a commodity that can be bought or sold.

There are a few pages in my book that I would like to rip out, but this is the deck that I was dealt, and the truth forced me to tell as it has happened.

I am not an advocate to tell people what they want to hear or what they need to hear, but leave them with the decision, if any one of them would fight women and children for the last seat on the lifeboat.

The book is based on real true happenings, but the names and places are fictitious to protect the innocent.

Zoltan Karpathy

Chapter I

A wedding has been called, many things: a union of two lovers, a promise to last for a lifetime, or the beginning of a dedicated loyal relationship, where two bodies, hearts and soul, meld as one.

It is also the definition for hope, future planning, and one might say: the optimistic dreaming, of life's happiness, that two people are destined to fulfill.

In Joe and Renay's life, it meant one more extra ingredient: freedom.

Both Joe and Renay, had grown up in orphanages since their parents had vanished, in the holocaust, that swept Europe, in the 1930's.

As the war came to an end, they each landed in America, where distant relatives gave them shelter, and education, but love was missing from their lives.

Joe finished his education in finance, and Renay in the field of teaching.

They met each other in the Senior year of college, and after a short period of time, learned about love: The love that they had for each other.

Their engagement preceded graduation, and shortly after graduation, they got married.

For the first time, they tasted real freedom: freedom to live, love, care, and plan for the future.

Because of their background, they wanted to have a large family, if they could afford it: and why not, Joe landed a great job with a local bank, and Renay found employment as a part-time teacher, with the promise of a full-time position, within a year.

Their prayers had been answered, in the form of Renay's pregnancy, and as the healthy girl child was born: they gave her the name "Anni."

Needless to say, they had an overflowing love, that they could not just please each other with, but also shared the love with their own flesh, and blood, that God gifted them with.

Anni was not pampered, but loved. Loved in the true sense of it's meaning.

Anni's parents were not only loving, but also intellectual enough, to recognize, that by the age of four, they had a gifted child on their hands.

Anni played very little with dolls, and showed a great interest in critters, piano, dancing in front of the television, and at five years of age, asked her parents for a toy called: "My Laboratory and Chemistry Shop."

At age six she began to receive lessons in piano, and ballet, and in the third grade, she received the first prize, for her concoction from her school for a chemistry project, that would have made the parents of a fourteen year old proud.

At the ripe age of ten, her father sat Anni down, for a heart-to-heart discussion. As the conversation took on a more serious course, Anni's father dropped the line: that knowledge is power. To his biggest surprise, Anni uttered, the following, remarkable sentence: "Daddy, I don't want the power of knowledge alone, but more so, the knowledge in power that translates, and relates, to the human species."

Skipping two years in high school: Anni graduated shortly after her sixteenth birthday, and left behind, not jealous, but countless good friends, to attend a prestigious university, that invited her one year prior to her graduation.

Anni enrolled for the studies of Biology, Psychology, and Sociology.

Her brilliant advancement was briefly interfered with, meeting a very handsome gentleman, from a prominent family, by the name of John Thompson.

This was one experience, that all the classes Anni took, did not prepare her for, and Anni fell in love with John.

John and Anni became an item, and spent most of their free time together.

Anni graduated with the highest honors, and both Anni and John received their Master Degrees.

Three months later, both of them being well employed, Mr. Thompson walked in, to Anni's parents house, with a bouquet of flowers, and recited the well anticipated sentence, that he desires Anni's hand in marriage, with the blessing of Joe and Renay.

A wedding is also called a meeting of the minds, and not just the bodies.

Neither Anni nor John could call each other, just a good catch, but more so, a double hooker.

John deserved Anni, and Anni admired John, for all the right reasons.

Their wedding was a well organized affair, that could have been written, in a story book romance novel.

Anni's parents were a respected couple in the community, and John's family, could boast, as being one of the most well-known, and well-off clan of the town.

John and Anni's marriage, however, did not bear the well-wished for fruit, in Anni's desire, to become pregnant. After numerous tries, and techniques, they both sought medical advice, and tests, to determine the reason, for their failure, of their marital bliss.

After numerous tests, it was diagnosed, that John's sperm count was too low, and practically unable to impregnate Anni.

Both Anni and John wanted to have children, and as two intellectual people, deep down inside, their secretive minds played, with numerous ideas, and possibilities, to achieve it.

One evening, as John and Anni visited the family restaurant, a couple sat in the next booth, and had with them, the most adorable toddler.

The longing, for the same was obviously sitting, on the faces of John and Anni, and their discussion, turned from food, to a more delicate subject.

Anni knew, that men are usually more shy, when it comes to admit their genetic makeup to reproduce, but the urge, to procreate, is the natural function of the female, and it was not different in John and Anni's case.

Taking an extra sip on her Chardonnay, Anni popped the often, yet awkward question directed at John. "Darling, have you ever thought about adoption?"

Anni knew, that the best, and strongest character in a man can usually withstand criticism for failure, to a certain degree, in success, looks, comprehension, talent, or communication. But when it comes to the ticklish subject of impotence, it blows the biggest hole, in the man's ego.

John visibly swallowed the dry saliva in his throat, and only after taking a good amount of wine, to lubricate his vocal chords, offered a response.

"Anni," he said: "I love you very much, and I would do anything to please you, not to mention be instrumental toward your desire, to have a child. But have you ever played, with the newly invented possibility of in vitro fertilization?"

"What a great idea," was Anni's reply. "Let's look into it darling, as soon as possible," she added.

After arriving home, that night, John made love to Anni, but on this occasion it was physically, and emotionally visible that he put everything in it: as to give an ultimatum to himself, and his unfounded guilty conscience, being inadequate to impregnate Anni.

A week later, Anni had her period, and it was obvious, that John's wonderful intention, ended in vain.

Anni's parents kept prying her, about a grandchild, but Anni was a very private person, and had not divulged the dilemma of John's shortcomings.

Anni thought: that a loving, caring, and committed relationship, that crowns itself in the form of a wedding, will nevertheless not escape, the good, or the bad side effect, of Destiny ... happiness, sadness, riches, poverty, sickness, or in some cases: tragedy.

Anni's parents, Joe and Renay, were getting ready, for their long planned, cross-country drive, and before they left, a dinner party was arranged, by Anni and John at their house.

The trip called, for a six week's absence, and the promise, that they will call twice a week, to report their whereabouts, and the adventures they experienced.

Joe and Renay were diligent, and true to their promise, and the phone rang two to three times, at Anni's home weekly, from them.

Then into the fourth week, Anni did not receive any call from her travelling parents, which made her antsy.

Anni registered her concern with John, whose reply was: "Darling: Maybe they're having such a good time, by themselves, that it skipped their mind to follow the routine, to check in with us."

Anni did not buy it. Her sixth sense echoed in her mind, that something was not kosher.

That night in bed, John noticed, that Anni had a very restless sleep and woke up several times.

At 7:00 a.m. the next morning, as Anni was pouring coffee, for John, and for herself: the front door bell rang, with a clang, that chilled Anni to her bones.

For some reason, they both went to the entry foyer, to answer the early intruder.

Opening the door, gave sight, of two uniformed State Troopers, and a civilian clothed distinguished gentleman.

"Mr. and Mrs. Thompson?" they asked.

Anni's heart dropped, like a lead balloon.

John answered: "Yes?"

"May we come in?" was the requested question.

"Of course," said John.

They were ushered into the living room, and a most awesome and frighteningly simple question, was raised from John: "What's wrong?"

Anni knew it, but could not avoid, hearing the monotone sentence, that never stopped ringing in her ears.

Mr. and Mrs. Thompson: "We are sorry to inform you, that Joe and Renay were involved, in a major car accident, with a gasoline truck, and all occupants perished, in that awful fire."

Anni silently told herself: Destiny?

Joe and Renay escaped the fire of the holocaust, only to end their lives, in a private one.

After some years, at a dinner party, Anni, with tears in her eyes, said to her friends: that she is a two time holocaust survivor.

They looked at her, with a bewildered gawk, and could not connect, her outburst, until she gave the perfect explanation, and the history of her parents.

A funeral is always a sad event, but in Anni's case, it meant the extinction of her family: since with the passing of her parents, she was now left, without any blood relatives.

The void in her life, carried the burden, that would have to rest, solely on her husband's shoulders.

John: Anni's husband, had the talent, and the compassion, to be equal to the task, not to mention, that they were practically still on their Honeymoon.

In order to pick up the shredded pieces of Anni's trauma: John became the most supportive, and compassionate, that Anni needed.

There were days, when John came home from his business, finding Anni sitting in a chair, with tearful eyes, and as a perfect confidant, he put her head on his shoulder, with a gentle hug, and without questions, told her: how much he loved her, and assured her, that time, and their love, would heal the wound, that was inflicted on Anni, by the loss of her parents.

The next morning, slowly gave way, to the grind, of everyday life, and Anni's thoughts, once again, started to concentrate, on the previous subject, of becoming pregnant.

The urge to procreate had become a more predominant issue, in her mental agenda: since the loss of her parents, and she told her husband, John, about her anguish, toward the goal of accomplishing it.

Countless days, and evenings, were consumed by the single subject, between Anni and John, as to how Anni could receive the gift of life in the form of a child.

Anni felt, that she had lost everything, by her parents death, and she desperately wanted to recoup her loss, no matter what it took, to produce her own offspring.

John suggested counselling, and after Anni's agreement, they sought out, one of the top professionals in the field.

After countless therapy sessions, mostly to John's benefit: a solid, but mildly controversial decision was reached: to start their research, for the appropriate steps, to fulfill Anni's function, as a possible candidate, for motherhood. Endless correspondence was followed up, by physical visits, and the all important final diagnosis, to accomplish, the medical miracle, that twenty five years ago, would have sounded: like a science fiction story; in vitro fertilization.

Anni had a very important and professional career in her field, and her employer, had the full understanding, not to mention the knowledge, of Anni's plight.

The cooperation, Anni received, from her supervisors for a leave of absence, played witness, as to how well regarded, and valued, Anni was to her firm.

Everything was ready and in place. The airplane tickets were secured, the luggage was packed, and the only thing that was left to do: was to travel toward the destination: that neither John nor Anni yet knew, for the future outcome.

Chapter II

Anni Thompson was now a thirty-nine-year-old college educated woman with a B.A. in Science and Technology. Her fifteen years of marriage to John Thompson, the CEO of a well-reputed conglomerate, ended in divorce a year ago. Shortly after marriage, the couple found out that Mr. Thompson's sperm count was too low to produce a child, and would not even be suitable for in-vitro fertilization.

After some agonizing discussions, the couple agreed to choose a well-reputed gynecologist whose anonymous gene pool came strictly from healthy, college-educated donors with above average I.Q.'s, and they were absolutely not traceable.

The procedure had been costly but both of the Thompsons came from middle-class families at the upper crust, and monetary issues played no role in their decision.

The gynecologist at the clinic where the procedure was performed paid tribute to this as the first procedure resulted in the pregnancy of Anni Thompson.

Anni was a very attractive, well-shaped woman with long, wavy auburn hair and green eyes. Her pregnancy accentuated her beauty. Her face would spell out "I am complete."

There were no complications, and nine months later the Thompsons received what they considered the greatest gift of their lives in the form of a girl baby, weighing eight pounds, six ounces.

Needless to say, the baby was pampered, and at the age of six attended parochial school and later high school.

The Thompsons gave their daughter the name of Erica, and without question, she inherited her mother's beauty and wit. The same could not be said for Mr. Thompson and, no wonder, he was not the biological father of Erica.

After their amicable divorce, Anni got a substantial settlement and purchased a condo in the best section of the city.

A year ago, she and her daughter, Erica, took residence in that condo.

Anni pursued her profession with the same firm and Erica continued high school and the hobby of softball as before.

Erica was the star pitcher of Coach Joe Cobb, and the many years of their affectionate and trusted relationship resulted in what one could describe as that of a substitute father and his adopted daughter.

Erica's mother, Anni, attended most of the games and sometimes even practices. Anni had known Joe Cobb for years, and trusted him with Erica in every situation.

Joe Cobb studied physical education and achieved the highest honors in the field. He is a six foot, one inch, forty-two-year-old guy with above average looks and intelligence, not too mention reputation.

Joe and Anni were on a first name basis, and sometimes even discussed issues beyond the perimeter of softball.

Once in a while, Anni dated professional colleagues outside of her employer's place, but never from where she worked. At one time, she even showed up at the softball practice with one of them.

The next time Anni went to the game, she was bold enough to ask Joe Cobb's opinion about her date.

Joe only raised one question to Anni: Is it serious?

Anni laughingly answered, of course not, and the subject never came up again between them.

Chapter III

It was a rainy day in July, and since Anni had a day off from work, and with Erica being on a six-day vacation to the coast to visit her father, she decided to be domestic and do the accumulated laundry.

Anni's first floor condo was right above the laundry room with a connecting utility room for electric and gas meters.

Anni was sitting in her living room sipping her coffee. She had a house dress on that buttoned from the top all the way down. Underneath, her well developed body was covered only with a bikini type cotton panty.

She was contemplating whether she should put a bra on before descending to the laundry room, but silently said: For what? It's only Wednesday and besides, nobody is home in the condos to observe her.

Stuffing the laundry in two pillowcases, along with the detergent, she grabbed her keys, clicked the door lock, and proceeded to the laundry room. There wasn't a soul around the hallway or in the laundry room and so, with a deep sigh, Anni felt perfectly safe.

Facing the wall where the machines were located, she opened the two top doors and selectively started to stuff the laundry into them.

Her task was interrupted with the noise of the entrance door being opened and, as she turned around to greet the possible neighbor, a masked man with a knife jumped her.

The man had extraordinary strength and, as he held the knife to her throat from behind, he put one hand on her mouth. He commanded her not to make a single noise or he would slit her throat. She frighteningly obeyed him and he opened the utility room door, dragging her in there. There was a bench in this room and snow shovels, also an old cot with a filthy mattress on it.

Holding the knife to her throat, he unbuttoned the first few top buttons of her house dress and then just ripped it off of her.

She was shaking, and begged for her life.

He forced her on that filthy mattress, ripped off her flimsy panties, and opened up his own zipper. Holding the knife with one hand to her delicate throat, he took out his penis with the other.

Anni closed her eyes at the sight of his immense anatomy and started to pray silently.

He knelt between her legs and penetrated her with a violent push. Her small vagina did not accommodate the maniac's penis under this involuntary act, and he raped her.

She was in agony, but fully aware that screaming would cause her death. Her silent prayers were partially answered as the perpetrator ejaculated into her in a couple of minutes.

After he finished his beastly act, she was told to turn around and lie face down on the mattress. He put some old rags on top of her head and told her not to look or make a sound or he would stab her to death.

Again, she started to pray and followed his commandments.

About two minutes later -- what seemed like two hours to her -- she did not hear a single noise or movement. Slowly she peaked out from under the rags. He was gone.

She put the half-ripped dress back on herself, pressed her ripped undies between her legs and against her bleeding vagina.

She stumbled upstairs to her condo and called 911.

Within five minutes, the police arrived with two detectives and a police woman. Shortly after the ambulance came also.

She described quickly to the officers what took place, and gave whatever description she could of the perpetrator. She started to feel physically ill and was put in the ambulance.

Minutes later, she was in the emergency room of the well-reputed local medical center. As destiny would have it, her attending physician was a lady doctor.

After a few preliminary questions, the doctor took swab samples, pubic hair samples, and all her clothes were put in a plastic bag to be preserved. She needed eight stitches to her anatomy, and was forced to stay in the hospital for three days.

The detectives came every day and bombarded her with numerous questions, some of them repeated ones. They told her that they have plenty of semen samples and were looking for possible witnesses.

On the last day of her hospital stay, Anni asked the detectives if they had found the guy or any witnesses, and so on. But, to her disappointment, she was informed that so far there was nothing, but they were working on it.

Chapter IV

After Anni was released from the hospital, she ordered a taxi since she didn't want the cops to take her home and create a scene, later to be explained to the neighbors.

As the taxi approached her condo, she hesitated, not wanting to get out, but she did. The taxi driver informed her that the fare was taken care of by the police department.

She quickly rushed to the front door, unlocked it, and sat down on her comfy couch. She started to wonder if she was safe or not in her own condo, but her intellect told her that she was not violated in her home. It was in the laundry below.

Her answering machine was full of messages, mainly from her daughter, Erica.

There is no way that she could have lied to her daughter about what had taken place, and so, as she returned the many unanswered calls from her, she calmly told Erica the truth.

The crying Erica informed Anni that she would interrupt her vacation and would take the next plane back home.

Anni tried to talk Erica out of it, but ex-husband John, got on the line and would take no refusal from Anni. As a matter of fact, John told Anni that even he will accompany Erica and take part in the unsolved case.

John explained to Anni, that he still knew important people in the county where she lived, and his connections could be put to good use, expediting the investigation.

In a split second, Anni's marriage to John, flashed in front of her, and the insisting character that John displayed during their marriage.

This time, however, her common sense told her, that it was a genuine concern, and she delegated this to John, with a thank you, and see you then. With that, she hung up the phone.

The knock on the front door scared Anni, but as she looked through the peephole, she was relieved. It was the two investigative detectives.

Anni right away had hopes that maybe some good news would be told to her. Instead, the two detectives informed her that the District Attorney's office would like to have a blood sample from Anni for D.N.A. testing, since they had already performed D.N.A. on the perpetrator's semen sample.

Anni was a little hesitant to agree, and she asked why it was necessary that her blood sample was needed.

The officers explained to her that the reason was two-fold. First, they found two types of blood in the D.N.A. sample of the perpetrator, and they wanted to make sure that one of them was Anni's. And secondly, to clear all venereal disease questions of either blood sample.

Anni agreed to donate the sample, and the detectives informed Anni that a registered nurse was waiting outside in the cop's car to perform the test.

Anni's ex-husband and Erica arrived the next day and, after expressing sympathy, John left to stay with his own relatives.

Erica was super-attentive to her mother the next couple of days, to the point that it bothered Anni.

Finally, Anni made Erica sit down and told her: "Look sweetheart, what happened happened. I'm not going to let this ruin my life and all the other lives around me. So please try to act normal, and let's go on with our everyday life so I can put this behind me. The more I'm reminded of it, the more it's going to hurt me. I like to think there's a possibility I can escape permanent emotional scarring from this trauma, and not become disabled for a life-time. So if you want to help me Erica, please do me a favor and let me ask for it."

Anni was always a very strong character, and her disciplined reasoning and constitution supplied her with a clear head and sound judgment. She knew that she had made a mistake by acting irresponsible as far as the laundry trip, but she failed to calculate that the price she paid would, or could be, as high as it turned out to be.

She had not considered the brutal act of rape as a possibility, yet told herself, that maybe if she would have been fully dressed, before going to the laundry room, maybe the perpetrator, would have had a harder time to carry out his beastly act, or even would have completely aborted it.

An inner voice told her that she was doing Monday morning quarterbacking, and the horrendous incident wasn't her fault, and it could never be the fault of any female.

As tears started to accumulate in her eyes, blurring her vision: she loudly declared, not to collapse under her emotional strain and cloud her otherwise sensible mind, and to take the next steps.

She also called her employer and, after a short explanation for her absence, her employer insisted on a paid, three week recovery period.

Anni was a performer in her professional field, and under no circumstance would her employer chance the possibility of losing her outstanding service to the firm. She even got an offer from her boss for maid service at his expense. It was nice to be that valued and appreciated.

She thanked him, but turned down the offer with the excuse that she found it easier to tolerate what happened by keeping busy, and was trying to pick up her normal routine as soon as possible.

"Anni, whatever you need is yours for the asking. Just call," her boss finally said. With that, the phone call was ended.

Anni thought that what she needed, was to be alone for a while and think. She needed to evaluate and analyze something, somebody, or herself, every waking hour of her life. This became directly or indirectly a fact of her life. No matter how ambivalent she became of the practice, she did it, consciously or subconsciously. No matter how intelligent and level headed Anni was, she could not escape the silent question she asked herself, "Where do I go from here?"

The difference between her existence and her life was that the latter was planned. Anni knew this, and a second silent question popped into her mind.

Is, or should, everything be a trade-off in life?

With the exception of force, accident, or an act of God, there were only two scenarios in existence whereby she formed her decisions. First, there was the outside influence of money, health, environment, friendship, love, or even religion and morals. The second one was the more powerful -- self conviction. The latter could contain some or all of the first or none of it.

It depended on how influenceable she was. If two people agree on everything, she thought, one of them is not needed.

The trick was to be able to reason with herself before she could reason with anybody else.

Anni was a very practical woman and a champ at this psyche. She knew from her past existence what would nourish her future one. Her sound judgment of do's and don'ts gave her an almost flawless guidance all of her life. She survived the devastation of divorce because of her two-timing husband. Divorce and rape had nothing in common, but Anni decided that she has been through the flames once, and she would also walk through the fire.

Chapter V

Weeks have passed by and not a single lead turned out to be profitable for the police. They had the perfect arsenal of proof well preserved in the laboratory of the crime unit, that any jury would view as the undeniable evidence, but no suspect.

Anni was back on her job, and for all outward appearances she seemed to have overcome the trauma.

The softball season was almost at hand, and the girls got notice to report for practice. After Erica's nagging and begging, Anni accompanied her to the first practice.

As soon as they arrived at the field, the coach, Joe Cobb rushed over and expressed his deepest sympathy to Anni, explaining that he just heard the awful news through the grapevine yesterday. He offered Anni anything at all to console her, or whatever he could do to help her.

Anni knew that he meant well, since the years of their acquaintance proved him to be genuine. She thanked him with a warm smile and stated that at least she did not feel uncomfortable with him knowing what happened.

He also mentioned that one day soon he would like to have a cup of coffee with her, in order to be more helpful to her in burying bad memories and creating new ones. Anni said she would like that.

He seconded the motion and jokingly said, "You have a date."

Erica overheard most of the conversation between Joe and Anni and raised the question. "Are you going to go out with him?"

Anni said, "I don't know. Maybe. Why? Do you have anything against it?"

Erica answered, "No, by all means. On the contrary."

They started to laugh, and only the coach's whistle to start the practice broke up their chuckle. As Erica ran to the field, Joe signalled Anni with a gesture that he would call her.

For obvious reasons, Anni slept better this night, and only the loud ringing of the phone late the next morning woke her up. It was Joe.

His voice sounded soothing in Anni's ears and, as he proposed to meet later for coffee, she said, "Okay."

Without giving Joe a second opportunity to name the time and place, Anni suggested the popular indoor/outdoor cafe a few blocks from the high school where Erica was attending and Joe was the coach. They set the time for three p.m. as it was convenient for both of their schedules.

Anni hung up the phone, took a deep breath, stretched out on her king size bed and, with a loud voice said, "Yes." She got out of bed and proceeded to the connecting shower room. She turned on the faucets and took a quick look in the full-size mirror that framed her matured body in profile. She turned, facing the mirror, and then again twisted her statuesque figure to view her backside. She coquettishly placed her index finger between her full lips. She started to smirk and then burst out laughing.

Putting her spider fingered hands on her thighs, she loudly declared, "Not bad, not bad at all."

Anni is not a stuffy lady, but in order to boost her ego, she silently made the following self confession: "I'm smart, well-educated, above-average looking with a well-developed figure. I'm still fairly young, with a good job, and a few bucks in the banks. Consensus is that I am easy going, and have a good attitude. People say that I have a lot of compassion for humanity, and for the kingdom of nature, and animals. I love sports, the theater, and was always judged as an excellent dancer. I have never been accused of upstaging anybody, especially my guys. Instead, I've been complimented from all sides as to how much fun it is to be with me.

So what do I have to worry about? I am what every eligible guy would want in my age group, right?

Finishing her synopsis, she took a final look in the by-now foggy mirror, but no inner voice gave her the reassuring answers that she was so adamantly searching for.

All of a sudden, bad memories crept back into her mind and she started to feel dirty.

She switched on the exhaust fan and stepped into the hot shower in the hope of cleaning her body and her mind.

Anni was known to all as a level-headed lady, almost to the point of being tough. But not tough in the sense of brute or rough, but experienced in most phases of life without a stuck-up nose. She had the talent to put people at ease, by not overpowering the other person with her sometimes superior intelligence. Friends and acquaintances valued her opinion, and more often than not, took her advice. She herself wondered who on earth could have wanted to hurt her in particular.

It has to be some form of a sub-human, she thought, resembling more a violent animal.

Anni stepped out of the shower, wrapped her terry coat around herself, went to the kitchen and started her pre-prepared coffee machine.

As she walked back to the master bedroom, her eyes fixed themselves on the grandfather clock in the hall. It was noon, and the Westminster chime correspondingly confirmed it.

Opening the mirrored double closet in the master bedroom, Anni stood in front of it, and tried to choose what to wear on her date.

All of a sudden, she started to laugh. "My God, I'm acting like a schoolgirl on her first date."

Then, like a dark cloud, her face hardened and she became very serious. "It's my first date. My first date after the rape."

Again, the agonizing questions played havoc in her mind. Will I ever get completely over it?

A few involuntary tears ran down on her high cheekbones, creating a picture of two miniature, oozing waterfalls as testimony to her damaged soul. But nobody, except Anni, could paint the tormented inside.

Her biggest quest would now be to master the strength and talent to paint over this picture. She figured that the first brush could be Joe, and with a delicate smile, she reached for a napkin and wiped away the tears that played witness to her inner agony.

She chose a pink jersey to wear with white sandals and a crocheted, long-strap pocketbook. As she tried on the outfit, she thought how complimentary her body and the dress were to each other.

At twenty minutes to three, Anni deliciously dressed, descended into her garage. She stepped into her red sports car, clicked on the automatic opener, and headed north on the boulevard toward the coffee house.

Chapter VI

While driving on the way toward her date, Anni's mind acted like a windmill that got caught in a tornado. Millions of questions popped into her mind, and the what-ifs play a violent ping-pong match in her brain.

Anni was a very careful driver and never had an accident, but on this occasion she had to admit to herself that she did not remember the route, or the red and green lights on the way to this meeting.

She took an open parking space right across from the coffee shop. She inserted two quarters into the meter, and spotted Joe sitting in the outdoor section of the establishment.

He had khaki, pleated canvas trousers on, complimented by a white polo shirt, brown leather-strapped sandals, and Porsche mirrored sunglasses. His dark, wavy, full head of hair had an extra sheen to it by the influence of brilliant sunshine.

They greeted each other by Joe saying how attractive she looked, and Anni repaying the compliment, saying "Thank you, so do you."

The waiter came right away, and Joe asked Anni what she would like. She chose cafe latte.

All Anni's previous experiences with dating just flew out the window, and she awkwardly felt like a mannequin on the main floor in the mall.

Before she could explain this phenomena, Joe opened up by saying: "So talk to me. What happened?"

Anni thought that Joe might have had a hidden agenda, and didn't want to be identified, and reveal the real target he was aiming for.

"What would you like to know?" Anni asked probingly.

Joe said, "Everything."

Anni flinched a little, but in a monotone voice she started to describe discreetly what had transpired, and told Joe about the so-far unsuccessful police investigation.

At this point, for some unexplainable reason, Anni felt for the first time uncomfortable, but she wasn't sure if the cause of her condition was Joe, or telling it to Joe, or the recurring memory.

Joe broke up her analytic thoughts by asking, "So what are you going to do?"

Anni felt that in order to regain balance in her life and in this conversation, she would insert some humor. "I can pick up the phone and, after the computer instruction, press five."

Joe looked a little bewildered and said, "What do you mean?"

Anni said "Just that. Nothing. There's nothing I can do but let time elapse and heal." Looking at Joe, Anni wondered if he wondered whether or not her elevator stopped on every floor.

Before she could say another word, Joe asked her if he could be part of the healing.

Everybody needs a little pat on the back, she thought. Nevertheless, she said, "Why would you want to be?"

Joe bluntly answered, "Because I care for you."

Anni didn't know why, but all of a sudden she felt undressed and completely naked in front of this attractive guy, and she had to admit that his compassionate declaration put this feeling in gear and stripped all the wheels in her brain. In her fantasy mind, she bumped her head with the palm of her hand, and made the following honest and well directed question to Joe.

"Okay, Joe, you seem to be telling me that you want to be my friend and confidant, who I'll be able to trust and believe in.

You're a very attractive man and, on the surface, there isn't a woman who wouldn't seek your company. But Joe, tell me, what, if anything, lurks beneath your beautiful facade?

"I'm not accusing or excusing you of anything, but if it's true that you care for me, slow down. Oh yes, one more thing, please promise to be honest with me no matter what, and I'll do the same."

Joe almost looked at her in a catatonic state, and as she finished, he took her hand and said, "Done."

She leaned over and put a delicate kiss on Joe's freshly shaved cheek.

Joe squeezed her piano fingers and asked for, and received, the next date.

On the way home, the buzzing in her head mimicked the Niagara Falls, and she was literally shaking like a sixteen-year-old girl who just encountered her first girl-guy talk and over-extended her curfew, and now had to answer to daddy.

As the garage door opened, she calmed down and knew that she had to answer to a much more critical person than her daddy -- to herself.

Chapter VII

Anni and Joe's relationship developed to a successful six month term, but they never had sex in the form of copulating. Anni respected this from Joe to the highest degree, but she also knew that pretty soon she would have to satisfy this healthy man's physical needs.

Everybody knew them as a steady couple, and their relationship was regarded with the highest respect from all friends, relatives, and acquaintances. Erica was practically in love with Joe, and acted with him like any fifteen-year-old would act toward mommy's gorgeous hunk.

One day, Erica felt a little under the weather, and Anni took her to her internist. He examined Erica and, not being able to make a diagnosis, recommended blood work.

Three days later, Erica turned for the worse, and Anni returned with her to the doctor. After a more lengthy examination, the doctor suggested that she be checked into the local medical center for various tests.

Anni and Erica went home, got the necessary stuff, and followed the doctor's order by checking Erica into the hospital.

Joe went the same night with Anni to visit Erica, and the picture at Erica's bed portrayed the perfect family union, with a sick daughter and a concerned mommy and daddy.

The doctor came in and informed Anni and Joe that the hospital would perform a liver bio on Erica, and also a D.N.A. from the bio, just in case. Needless to say, the unfavorable news weighed heavily on Anni and Joe, but they had no choice in the matter. It had to be done.

Two days later, the bio tests came back, and Erica's illness wasn't as serious as first suspected. The doctor reassured Anni that the drug therapy treatment would free Erica from her affliction, and with time she would completely recover.

The doctor also informed Anni that they would preserve the D.N.A. results, just in case the liver should act up again, and a transplant would be necessary.

Anni thanked her long-time friend and doctor, and gave him a warm hug, saying, "What would I do without you."

Two days later, Erica left the hospital and resumed her normal activities.

Anni kept a careful and vigilant eye on her but, after a while, as she did not show any relapse, Anni practiced her previous easy-going attitude with Erica.

Joe had returned more often, and they started to go out even more frequently than before.

On one occasion, as Anni was shopping in the local mall, she ran across the social worker who offered rape counseling to Anni at the time of her trauma. But Anni refused the offer for the reason that it would just keep the wound open and her bad memories alive.

The social worker asked Anni how things were going, and Anni replied gingerly that things were getting better, and she'd even started a relationship with a reputable gentleman.

After some less significant chit chat, they parted company with the reassurance from the social worker that if Anni should ever need her, she knew where to find her.

The accidental meeting again brought back haunting memories for Anni, and to soothe her slightly upset stomach, she chose to sit down at the mall's coffee shop with a cup of coffee. She was sitting right next to the glass wall that gave a completely full view of the passersby's. For the first time in her life, she started to analyze the crowd as a whole, and then individually. A self-accusatory question started to creep in on her mind.

Why do I do this? I've never done this before. Then the doubting voice in her said: Maybe I should have taken advantage six months ago of the suggested rape counseling. Then she started to entertain the thought that maybe even after six months, it would be to her advantage.

She must have been sitting there quite a while, because as she reached for her cup, she noticed a dark ring slightly above the level of the remaining coffee. She put the cup down, shook her head, left a tip on the small table, and forced herself between the bustling crowd.

As she was walking almost aimlessly, a bitter smile surfaced on her otherwise flawless face. Her inner voice formulated a sentence, nobody said it's going to be easy.

After all the hundreds of reassurance from Joe, Anni felt that something was still missing. She debated within herself, trying to put her finger on it.

She was brought back to present reality as she looked at her watch and noticed that the beauty parlor appointment that she was scheduled for was barely thirty minutes ahead.

She aimed for the mall exit, and arrived just in time for her treatment at the hair salon. She was greeted by the owner with a peck on her cheek, since she was not only her beautician, but also a long time good friend.

No sooner than she was ushered to a semi-private station, the friend asked her: "So how are things going?"

Anni felt that the question from her friend wasn't placed in a concerned fashion. For some reason, Anni felt snippy and answered her with a question: "Comparing to what?"

Her friend's face turned, and with an apologetic voice she said, "I'm sorry, I didn't mean it that way. I haven't seen you for a while, and you should know by now that you have a place in my heart."

Anni acknowledged inside of herself that this is the second unknown phenomena she was experiencing today, and she felt a gross amount of insecurity inside. She looked at her friend, gave a warm touch to her hand and said, "Please, don't get mad at me. It's not you, it's me."

Her friend, the beautician, had been married three times, and when it came to marriage and divorce, or relationships, she could conduct a seminar. She opened up like a psychotherapist. "You know," she said to Anni, "you need to wake up, smell the coffee, and get rid of the freeze dried."

As she coined the phrases, Anni thought that maybe she's trying to insert some humor in their conversation, so she asked, "What are you trying to say?"

Her friend replied, "Look, I have no monopoly on free advice, but if I were you, I'd eliminate all impossibilities. Whatever remains, however impossible it is, is the truth."

Anni was even more confused than before, and registered her bewilderment to her friend. In an almost begging voice, she asked her friend to put it in a layman's term what she meant.

"All right," replied the friend. Listen to me. We all live between two worlds -- one on the outside and one on the inside. What you're portraying on the outside would fake out anybody to the point that there's nothing bothering you. But I know you and I know better. Your inside world resembles World War III, and don't try to deny it.

"Tell me, am I wrong?"

Anni just looked down and had to admit to herself how well her friend knew her.

Her friend did not give Anni a chance to even confess to her silent agreement, but went on. "Don't let me shake the trees and see what falls out from the branches. I'm your friend, and you know you can trust me under any circumstance. And whatever you tell me, it stays right here between the two of us."

Anni's twitching face gave witness to the fact that there are fixed laws in nature. Any further play-acting would have been useless, and as her heart increased in palpitation, she recognized that her long-time friend's talent was equal to a psychiatrist who might use rationality psychoanalysis to explain reality.

Her friend went on just like a pro. "You see, expectancy will cure you or make you ill. It's called a slight mental imbalance. Willingness is an agreement, or giving up one's own will. It's also brainwashing from an outside source. We're not born with the instinct to trust. It has to be earned. I think I earned yours, didn't I?"

Anni just answered with a shaky voice, "Of course."

"Well then, talk to me," said the trusted friend.

Anni smiled and became like a drunken spy who, under vigorous torture, regurgitates the whole truth and then some.

When she finished, she also added, "So there, you have the whole truth from A to Z."

Anni's friend dropped the scissors and comb from her hands, and with a strong hug embraced Anni. "That's better," she said, "now you have an ally on your side that's honest, without any material, sexual, or moral interest.

"Now we'll fight and we'll win. Now there's the two of us. You're not alone any more in this. I'm swearing an alliance to you, that no matter what, I'll be on your side, whenever, whatever, and wherever you need me."

As Anni left the beauty salon, she felt that she had just unloaded 200 pounds of weight after carrying it for six months.

Chapter VIII

Arriving home, Anni made for herself a stiff Manhattan and propped herself in the easy chair in front of the fireplace.

As she fixed her eyes on the huge painting portraying a Mexican toreador and a charging bull that decorated the wall above, she thought about all the words that her friend told her. In a loud voice, raising her glass, Anni declared, "Yes, I'll fight to the bitter end to find this bastard who violated every physical and moral standard that I stand for. And if that's the last thing I do in my life, I'll make him pay for it."

She felt stronger, freer, bolder and definitely focused. She almost assumed a chameleon-like look. She needed it, since tonight was the big date with Joe, to the wedding party of his niece.

She looked at the clock. It was one p.m. and Joe was supposed to pick her up at three thirty for the four o'clock ceremony.

After a hot bubble bath in her jacuzzi, she applied the perfect makeup and slipped into a black-lace, one-piece lingerie with a garter belt to secure the hazy black stockings that covered her long, well-developed, and well-formed tan legs.

The red Georgette dress was complemented with black patent leather high heels and matching pocketbook. She forced her long fingered hands into a three-quarter length Napa gloves, and a silver fox shoulder cape finished the picture.

She looked in the full-size mirror, threw herself a kiss and remarked, "You look marvelous."

The chime sounded off to her entrance door and, as she answered the intercom, the friendly voice on the other end was Mr. Joe Cobb for Ms. Anni Thompson.

Anni laughed and answered, "I'll be down in a minute."

His attire consisted of a pigeon gray tuxedo with matching shoes, white ruffled shirt, and a pink bow-tie with matching hankie. His dark wavy hair and piercing blue eyes were even more predominant than before, and Anni had to admit that he looked very tempting.

He presented her with a tender kiss on the cheek, a corsage, and a compliment that would sweep any healthy woman off her feet.

They got into Joe's black Cadillac, and as they arrived at the church a few minutes early, everybody greeted them with hugs, kisses, and compliments.

It was a well-organized, formal wedding, and everybody who was anybody important in the city was invited and attended the wedding, as the Cobbs were very influential and a politically well connected family.

The reception that followed took place in the famous hotel's grand ballroom. A nine-piece live band entertained the guests, and the waiters, with white-glove service and strolling with appetizer trays, offered champagne to the guests.

After the introductions and the best man's speech, the wedding party started the traditional dances, and then invited the rest of the crowd to participate.

Joe stood up, made a deep bow in front of Anni, and said, "May I have the honor?"

Anni smiled, got up, and replied "With pleasure."

As they walked toward the dance floor, Anni felt that every eye in the room was fixed on her.

As the dance ended, and they were walking back to their table, applauding people focused toward them. One of them said, "Beautiful, lovely, what a good looking couple."

Anni couldn't remember the last time she felt embarrassed or flushed in the face, as she did on this occasion.

Joe pulled her chair out for her to sit down, and whispered in her ear, "Let them eat their hearts out."

The dinner arrived after numerous cocktails, and Anni appreciated the food since she started to feel a little lightheaded. Joe was also a touch more friskier than usual.

After dessert, coffee and a couple more after-dinner drinks, the party started to disassemble. After saying goodbyes, Anni and Joe followed suit.

They were giggling all the way home, and as Joe parked his car in the condo's visiting lot, he raised the expected, but dreaded, question. "Don't I deserve a nice brandy for a nightcap? And by the way, I've never seen your place inside."

Anni knew that this was the moment of make it or break it in this relationship. She would reveal away either way as to whether she trusted Joe or not. So she answered with a casual voice, "By all means, even two."

They both entered Anni's condo and, as she clicked the door lock, Joe gently caressed her from the back, turned her around, and put his lips on hers.

After a long and passionate kiss, he whispered in her ear, "Tonight, you're mine."

Anni was slightly turned on, but her brain started a war with her physical desire.

Joe did not give her a second chance to respond, and her silence was translated to willingness in Joe's mind. He picked her up and carried her into the bedroom which was visible since the folding doors were open. He gently laid her down on the king-size bed, kissed her lips one more time, and started to feel her legs and breasts.

A minute later, he unbuttoned her dress and freed her from it.

Reaching for her snap on the front of the bra gave sight to Anni's firm, well-developed chest, and her nipples were hard and enlarged. He caressed them with his hands and lips while slipping down the rest of her lingerie, except the garter belt and the stockings.

Anni just laid there practically motionless, like the marble statue of the <u>Venus de Milo</u>. As he raised himself slightly to remove his attire, Anni said in a shaky voice, "Please be careful. You know, this is the first time after my misfortune that I'm doing this."

Resting on one of his elbows, he opened up her legs, touched her full vagina, and the by now protruded clitoris and, putting his lips on hers, started to mount her.

He began to penetrate her, but Anni started to moan as his over-sized penis wasn't successful to plunge into her. She asked him to wait, but he wouldn't.

Instead of listening to her, he forced his penis into her with a violent push, and started to pump with a frenzy. Anni screamed out loud and begged him to stop because he was hurting her.

But he wouldn't.

Anni felt physically groped and she well remembered the scene six months earlier. She knew who this guy was. She knew that the man she let in her life and confidence was no other than the beast who had raped her. Then everything came crushing down on her.

Could it be possible that she was making a nightmarish mistake? Is it reasonable to believe that there are two guys built exactly the same, and behave the same when they perform sexually?

She ordered him to stop but she didn't even finish uttering her last word as he ejaculated in her.

He pulled out of her and wanted to kiss her, but she refused, and in a mad voice told him to get his stuff and leave.

He said, "What's the matter? Are you crazy?"

"No," she said. "For the first time in my life, I'm positively smart. So get out."

He threw his clothes on himself and left.

Anni closed the door and grabbed the telephone.

As the Police Department answered on the other end, she asked for the two detectives who six or seven months ago had handled her rape case.

The sergeant informed Anni that neither one of them was available, as they were off duty and, at this hour, probably home sleeping.

She said to the sergeant to call one of them and wake him up. "Tell him that I'm Anni Thompson and my rapist just left my home."

The sergeant said, "Yes ma'am, what's your number?"

She told him and hung up.

Chapter IX

No more than five minutes later, Anni's phone rang. It was the detective.

Anni told him her story, and the detective told Anni to lay down and to not clean herself, as he would be there in fifteen minutes with a woman police nurse.

They arrived promptly, and the nurse took Anni to the hospital where they performed the swabbing and all the necessary tests that they would do under the circumstances of rape.

Talk about the ultimate nightmare -- making love to your long lost rapist. Anni was laying on her hospital bed and the thought made her throw up.

She rang the nurse and the doctor came in as well. The nurse cleaned her up and the doctor administered a powerful sedative that put Anni to sleep until late the next morning.

The detective interviewed Anni at the hospital and told the doctors to detain her overnight for observation. He also ordered a cop to her room and a cop car to her condo, just in case.

He left Anni's bedside and went directly to the telephone.

The judge wasn't too happy to be awakened at such an early hour of the night. But when the detective told him the whole history of the case, he was more than willing to meet the cop, upon which the judge issued a search warrant of Mr. Joe Cobb's residence, and also a warrant for his arrest.

As the doorbell rang at the well-known residence of the Cobb family, a tall, good looking gentleman answered it, and faced the two detectives.

They greeted him and asked him if he was Mr. Joe Cobb.

He said, "Yes. What seems to be the problem?"

They just took out the handcuffs and said "Mr. Joe Cobb, you're under arrest for the rape, kidnapping, and sexual misconduct of Miss Anni Thompson. You have the right to be silent and anything you say could and will be held against you." The cop finished the reading of the Miranda in usual fashion.

With that, they cuffed him and took him downtown to the police headquarters, where he was photographed and fingerprinted. When they asked him if he would like to give a statement, he refused and demanded his lawyer be present. They accommodated him with a telephone and he was successful in reaching his attorney.

An hour later, the attorney arrived, and he told the two detectives on whose behalf he was appearing. The detectives looked at each other, because this attorney was the most famous and well-reputed defense attorney in the State, and may have even been among the top five in the country.

"I'm here to see my client, Mr. Joe Cobb."

Joe was soon instructed not to say a word to anybody, and wait until the next morning when the formal arraignment would take place in the courtroom in front of the judge.

The next morning, Joe Cobb, with his super attorney, was standing in front of the judge and the prosecutor.

The prosecutor read the charge and asked the judge to detain Mr. Joe Cobb in the local jail until the preliminary hearing.

The Judge asked the accused how he pleaded.

Joe Cobb stated with a loud and clear voice, "Absolutely not guilty."

Then the prosecutor stood up again and requested from the Judge to set a bail at one million dollars, since the Cobb family was very well heeled and the possibility of flight existed.

The famous attorney jumped from his seat and said, "Your Honor, the District Attorney is completely out of line. My client is an upstanding citizen of this county without any prior record, and it would be completely out of line to burden him with this huge amount of bail."

The Judge agreed and reduced the bail to two hundred and fifty thousand dollars.

The preliminary hearing was scheduled by the judge within thirty days, but again the defending attorney's plea to the judge as to the case and charge being a very complicated and serious situation, moved the judge to agree to a sixty day term.

Joe's attorney arranged bail and, within an hour, Mr. Joe Cobb was a temporary free man, roaming the city streets with his black Cadillac.

Anni woke up to the friendly voice of the attending nurse. "It's breakfast, darling, how do you feel?"

"Like a Mack truck hit me," she replied.

"That's all right," remarked the nurse. "You'll feel much better after breakfast."

Anni had just swallowed her last desirable piece of food as the District Attorney came into her room with the detective.

The District Attorney introduced herself and stated the reason for her appearance. She informed Anni that she would use a tape recorder, with Anni's permission, and use the detective as a witness to the proceedings.

Anni agreed to all the conditions and the D.A. started by reciting her name, time, and Anni's full name, and the detective's full name, before the inquiry began.

Anni told them the whole story, and after switching the tape recorder off, the D.A. remarked to Anni that, in a way, it looked like an open and shut case.

As the investigating party departed, Anni picked up the receiver from her bedside phone and called her friend, Helen, from the beauty parlor.

After a brief retelling of events, Helen told Anni that she'd be over in thirty minutes. As Anni was waiting for

Helen, she made a second, more uncomfortable call to her employer and explained her situation to the firm's executive.

Helen greeted Anni on her arrival with stretched out arms, as if to say: Honey, you have nothing to worry about, I'm here to take charge, and everything is going to be all right.

Without any delay, Helen's five minute speech was an uninterrupted declaration that she had recruited herself in the war that was silently brewing between Anni Thompson and Joe Cobb.

Helen also said that under no circumstance should Anni return to her condo, but instead to one of her relative's two counties away, where Erica would also be safe from any harassment. Anni agreed, and Helen called Erica to stay overnight in her house.

The bad news had not yet reached Erica, since she was spending three days and two nights with her best girlfriend's parent's house at the shore.

Chapter X

Helen had to use all her wits to convince Erica on the phone about what had happened.

Erica was snipping back at Helen by saying, "Look, I'm not the best judge of character, but I can't believe we're talking about the same Joe Cobb."

Helen got frustrated and told Erica, "If you have an I.Q. above an eggplant, you'll listen to me and come home on the double."

"It's your mother's wish also, but don't go to the hospital, come directly to my house."

Erica finally agreed that she'd be there the same day, late afternoon, at Helen's house.

Helen hung up the phone and said to herself, "Some guys act tough like they have a tattoo on their dick." In her thoughts, she was referring to Joe Cobb. Those demented dimwits cause all the problems, and to top it off, now even Erica will have to recover from her devotion to Joe. Helen also silently added, "I need a Tetanus shot just to think about it."

Helen knew that girls at Erica's age were very impressionable, and sometimes look for instant gratification.

When she and Erica started to take things apart that afternoon, Helen bluntly told Erica, "Look, I have underwear older than you, and experience that you haven't even read about. So take my word for it, this guy's dirty."

Helen was a kind but very tough lady. When she put her mind to something, she adopted the method of good, better, and best, but never let it rest.

She called the shots as she saw them, and never tried to redefine anything. She wouldn't put up with any nonsense and asinine possibilities simply did not exist in her mind. She always gave at least as much as she received and never let things get out of balance. She was very understanding, but if pushed, she would push back. She believed that the only healthy love was when they love you back.

She was very capable to defend herself under any pressure and situation. This was probably the reason that she had three marriages behind her, and didn't believe in Freud's theory that what a woman wants is mostly biological, and that what men want most is a best friend.

She was married to three losers, and had adopted the cockroach theory that you seldom see just one. Because of her masculine attitude, and direct approach, she had been told on numerous occasions, by her friends that she would make a more befitting husband for most of the opposite gender.

She believed that men never got tired of talking about themselves, and most of them loved every woman. Talk about two imperfect genders -- put them together and you get one imperfect relationship, she now thought.

The ringing of the phone broke up Helen's therapeutic speech to Erica.

The insecure voice on the other end of the line was Anni's. She said, humorously, "It's me, the damaged goods."

Helen informed her that she'd be over the next morning to pick up Anni, since the doctors gave her the green light to leave the hospital.

Erica accompanied Helen to the hospital, and all three of them went back to Helen's house to formulate a war plan to deball Mr. Cobb.

At home, Helen said to Anni, that she had searched for a suitable partner, and never found the real McCoy. She further went on to say that once in a while, a genuine one comes along, and most of the time people don't even recognize his or her existence. Then Helen confessed that sometimes her own feelings tore her apart, and she didn't know what to do with them. She felt like she wanted to throw them away, or she wanted to throw herself away.

Helen further remarked that she believed that some things come often in a lifetime. Some things come only once.

Sometimes you want to let it go and you can't.

Sometimes we are trying to act like someone else, yet that is the time when we recognize that we are more of ourself than ever before.

Helen stated that she was convinced that obsessions have no reasons. That is why they are called obsessions.

Then turning toward Anni, Helen said the following: "Joe Cobb and his imposed morality on you Anni, is equal to the rotten attitude of a mutated sub-species. To have trampled on your soul with his forceful agenda, was the Devil's work in him. No question about it, sooner or later, he will burn for it. His eroded mind is barely worth the bullet to his brain. I am sure that his reservation in Hell has been confirmed from his boss, the Devil."

Then with a visible sigh, Helen stopped talking.

A loud silence filled the room at Helen's house where the three ladies converged for one reason.

Anni called the D.A.'s Office and told the prosecuting lady lawyer her new temporary residence and phone number. She also asked the D.A. to tell the two detectives the same.

Helen called a conference between the ladies and, turning toward Anni, said, "You prove yourself by your actions, and not by what you're saying."

Anni learned lately that adversity is nothing compared to her pride. Thinking back on what Joe Cobb did to her, all the feelings of mercy left Anni's compassion and her silent confession said, this guy is a snake in the disguise of an angel.

She decided that the loss that she suffered from Joe Cobb's action only made her stronger.

There was nothing really that could have made Anni ready for the experience that happened but, without exception, it made her harder, and the ardent feeling of revenge became the main occupation of her thinking method.

Anni without any further ado, loudly declared to her co-conspirators that she was ready.

Helen said that some plans were based on one or more cold facts, and some are changed as circumstances alter. Anni's flight was more closely related to the latter, as Anni was ready for anything and everything, or so she thought.

Giving up, even after some unforeseeable setback, was excluded from Anni's fundamental belief. She swore to herself that she would get this guy, no matter what it took.

Chapter XI

The date of the trial of the State versus Mr. Joe Cobb on the charge of Miss Anni Thompson had been set, and all participants were sent notices in the form of subpoenas to appear.

The names of Anni Thompson and Joe Cobb became household names as the newspapers and the television reported almost on a daily basis as the case developed. In all the bars, coffee houses and living rooms, the main subject of discussion was mostly, and almost exclusively, the case of Anni Thompson and Joe Cobb.

The country formed an imaginary jury, whereby their for and/or against opinions changed on a daily basis. One couldn't even meet by accident on the street without at least raising the question from one or the other as to what you think of the case of Miss Thompson and Mr. Cobb.

It has semi-paralyzed the country, at least emotionally, but to some extent also economically. Some people even skipped other forms of entertainment just to read or listen to the latest news involving the matter. The anticipation was even more hyped as the Judge agreed to let the T.V. cameras in for the upcoming trial.

Bookies were taking bets and offered different odds for different verdicts. The country was in a frenzy. Even before the trial started, the reporters tried to bombard various potential witnesses with countless questions.

But Anni and Helen had a brilliant foresight by design, and escaped the sharks attempt to find them. Anni took Erica out of her school and hired a private tutor.

She also got an agreement with her employer to take an unpaid leave of absence from her job until the case concludes to a verdict.

So far, everything seemed to be working out to Anni's advantage, and all signs pointed favorably toward the rightful crucifixion of the accused, Mr. Cobb.

Chapter XII

Finally, it was Monday morning, and the well-advanced advertised date for the beginning of the trial.

A brilliant sunshine descended on the crowd and the countless reporters, T.V. cameras and crew that gathered in front of the Superior Courthouse well in advance for the 9 a.m. start of the trial.

As the D.A. entered the building, the reporters mobbed her with microphones pushed into her face, and the numerous questions came. Each time some new witness approached the courthouse, the same frenzy continued.

As the accused, Mr. Joe Cobb, with his famous attorney, Mr. Bentley, was seen getting out from their car, the crowd started to scream with a mixture of boos and a few applauses.

One of the famous T.V. anchormen got close to Mr. Cobb and his attorney, and raised the most simple but, at the same time, accusatory question. "Did you do it?"

Mr. Cobb didn't even raise his head, but his attorney said, "No comment."

The cops forcefully opened an aisle in the mob to give access for the defendant to go into the courthouse.

After some additional witnesses appeared, the crowd burst out in a loud applause that resembled the approval for a touchdown at the Super Bowl. This outburst was contributed to the arrival of Anni Thompson and Helen.

The same T.V. anchorman who asked the question of Joe Cobb was again fortunate to get close to the two ladies, and asked Anni, "How do you feel?"

Anni couldn't even open her mouth as Helen replied to the anchorman. "He will burn!"

Inside the courtroom, it looked like a hornet's nest. The defending attorney's table on the left and the plaintiff's D.A. table on the right were separated from the crowd with a fancy wooden gate, and with only a four foot opening on each side from the walls of the huge courtroom. The T.V. cameras were installed a day before under the rules and regulations of the presiding Judge.

The jury of seven women and five men, with six alternates, had been selected, and safely tucked away upstairs in a jury room.

The crowd was so loud in the benches that one could barely even hear one's own voice. It was 9:30 a.m. and the Judge, with two opposing attorneys, was still in his chamber, probably to iron out some final legalities. Finally, at about 10 a.m. the Bailiff, using the microphone, alerted the crowd to be seated and to be quiet.

Everybody sat down and an eerie silence filled the room as the Judge walked into the courtroom and took his seat.

Joe Cobb, with his attorney, Mr. Bentley, and Anni Thompson with the D.A., Miss Slater, rose from their chairs. And so did the crowd, on the order of the Bailiff.

The Judge, with a pleasant but very firm voice, told the crowd and the participants for the trial to please be seated. The Judge asked the D.A., Miss Slater, if she would like to ask him for anything before he called in the jury.

She answered, "No, your Honor, we are ready."

The Judge then turned toward the defending attorney, Mr. Bentley.

Mr. Bentley got up and simply gave the answer, "Ready, your honor."

Anni and the D.A. together had been previously interviewed by the Judge in regard to the publicity and whether she would not want her face to be shown on the T.V.

Anni said, "No, your Honor, I want the whole world to see the scarring and hear the truth of what this man did to me, to my body, to my soul, to my health, to my reputation, and to my future."

Anni had satisfied the Judge's concern and the T.V. cameras were installed.

Now, some murmuring took place in the crowd and the Judge practiced his lawful given right by gently slamming his gavel to its plate. "Order in the court," said the Judge, and he reminded the crowd that he would not tolerate any talking or outbursts from them, and he would not hesitate to clear the room for the rest of the proceedings.

That cured the crowd's behavior, and a dead silence set into the courtroom.

The Judge instructed the Bailiff to please bring in the jury.

The jury marched into the room toward their appointed seats. After the jury and the standing participants were seated, the Judge read off the charge to the jury and had a lengthy instruction for them.

As he inquired of the jury whether or not they have understood everything so far, he received a resounding "Yes" from them. Then the Judge asked them whether or not they had selected a foreperson for their future deliberations.

A very dignified tall lady with silver-gray hair and gold wired glasses stood up from her chair and answered to the Judge: "Yes, your Honor. I'm the fortunate or unfortunate one who was chosen to keep order between us."

Then the Judge informed the forelady of her duties and role, and thanked her.

Looking at the D.A., the Judge asked her if she was ready for her opening statement.

She answered, "Yes, your Honor."

The Judge said one more simple, inviting sentence. "At your leisure, Miss Slater."

Miss Slater walked out from beyond her table, ever so slightly pushing her chair back. She was attired with a dark gray business suit and high heels. Her short and gently waved blonde hair framed a stern, but a very reassured intellectual's face. She was a fifty-two-year old, practiced experienced fox, and really looked only forty-two.

In a slow, but deliberate walk toward the jury, she greeted them and expressed her appreciation for the enormous tasks that they would have ahead of them deciding the case. After these usual formalities, she changed her tone of voice as she opened up her statement with the following sentence.

"Ladies and gentlemen of the jury, this is the case of the State on behalf of Miss Anni Thompson, versus the defendant, Mr. Joe Cobb. We will prove beyond any doubt that on that fateful day of Wednesday in July, the defendant, Mr. Joe Cobb, with forethought, forcefully and maliciously attacked, kidnapped, and raped the plaintiff, Miss Anni Thompson, in the laundry room and in the adjoining utility room under Miss Thompson's condo.

"We will also prove beyond any doubt that that perpetrator is no other than the defendant, Mr. Joe Cobb."

"We will produce countless evidence, D.N.A. test results, and witnesses to establish his guilt. Your job will be to determine his innocence or guilt by listening carefully to all the witnesses and evaluating the overwhelming evidence before you come to a unanimous verdict. Please do not form any opinion before the whole case is finished and presented to you."

"After presenting our case to you, we'll ask you to find the defendant guilty as charged and impose the maximum punishment for this sub-human, animalistic crime that he committed against the law and Miss Anni Thompson."

"Again, ladies and gentlemen, I thank you for your indulgence, ask you to be attentive to the proceedings, and let your guidance be the merit of the case without being influenced by any other personal feelings of bias toward the participants. Thank you."

As she returned to her chair, the jury turned their focus toward the Judge, who was looking at his watch and declared that it was close to lunchtime. He informed all that he was calling for a lunch break. He also informed the attorneys and their clients to return by two o'clock to continue.

After that, he warned the jury not to form any opinion or discuss the case amongst each other until all the proceedings are concluded. The jury was dismissed. After the Judge left the courtroom in front of the standing crowd and the participants, a deafening noise reoccurred as before the trial.

Chapter XIII

Joe Cobb and Mr. Bentley left first. And then in the company of Miss Slater, Anni and Helen went to the close-by popular eatery.

They chose the available private corner table and Miss Slater took a seat by the wall in order to observe the incoming guests, just in case someone would come too close to their table and overhear any discussion that took place.

The waitress came to take their order, and when it was Anni's turn she said she just wanted a cup of coffee, since her stomach was upset by seeing Mr. Cobb again in the courtroom.

Helen said "No way, I'm not going to let you get sick by not eating. At least order the special beef barley soup. It's easy to digest and hearty enough to hold you."

Miss Slater smilingly agreed, and Anni took their advice.

As the waitress left, the first question came from Anni. Looking at the D.A., she said, "So how do you like the mixture and attitude of the jury?"

"Well," Miss Slater said, "You never know how the jury feels, or who they favor. In all of my practice, I could never figure out most of the juries, so I gave up on it. What I've learned is that if I present my case in a clear and decisive manner, I usually come out on the top and get the result that I'm looking for."

Helen rudely put her two cents into the conversation by saying, "You mean it's like a crap shoot?"

Miss Slater was smiling and said to Helen, "In a way, yes, but we have a very strong case with overwhelming evidence. I'm sure that the jury will see it the same way." At this, the D.A. looked at her watch and said, "My God, it's one-thirty. We'd better start going back."

Anni took the check, but the D.A. said, "No way, I'll take care of that."

Helen cynically thought, Sure, why not? It'll be charged to Anni's expenses under some cockamamie column.

The courtroom was already full as the D.A. and the two ladies arrived. They took their appointed chairs and ten minutes later the Bailiff practiced his previous duty by telling the crowd to stand and be quiet. They obeyed, and after they brought in the jury the Judge walked in.

"Please be seated," he said. Then he continued with his usual legalese by saying that this was the continuation of the State on behalf of the plaintiff, Miss Anni Thompson versus the defendant, Mr. Joe Cobb. With that, he turned toward the defendant's table and invitingly said, "Mr. Bentley, at your leisure."

This famous attorney, who had the finest reputation, and was very highly regarded in the judicial system as one of the best, if not the very best, rose from his chair. As he stood up, his six feet two inch well-postured shape resembled Clark Gable in looks, and an ex-college dean in behavior.

His attractiveness almost overshadowed Joe Cobb's, but not quite. They were a team that looked like movie stars acting out a role. You couldn't help but be impressed at least by their appearance.

Mr. Bentley put his hands together in a praying fashion and, with an abrupt walk, approached the jury. "Good afternoon, ladies and gentlemen," he started with his usual charm. "I hope all of you had an enjoyable lunch and are ready to dismiss all the charges against my client."

The jury started to smile, and the whole crowd burst out in loud laughter.

The Judge performed his duty by using his gavel, and then turning toward Mr. Bentley said, "Mr. Bentley, please don't entice the jury and the crowd by turning my courtroom into a circus."

Mr. Bentley said, "I apologize, your Honor."

The Judge's reply was, "Please proceed."

Mr. Bentley turned back to the jury, disconnected his praying hands, reversed them to his back, and clutched them again in a hook form. His voice was raised a couple of decibels and sounded very purposeful. "Ladies and gentlemen. My client, Mr. Joe Cobb, is innocent of all of the charges that the D.A. told you. We are vehemently denying all of the accusations to be true as far as Mr. Cobb's participation.

We will prove beyond any doubt to you that the person who committed this awful, and I might say sub-human act, is someone other than Mr. Cobb. And at the end of the proceedings you'll have no choice but to be convinced, like I am, that Mr. Cobb is as innocent of the charges as any one of you people sitting in the jury box.

"We will prove to you that this felonious charge of the D.A. is a complete fairy tale in bad taste, and our main and only concern is Mr. Cobb's future reputation after you find him innocent of all charges. Thank you ladies and gentlemen." He sat down, and his face looked satisfied.

The Judge turned toward the D.A. and raised the question that really signalled the beginning of the trial. "Miss Slater, are you ready to call your first witness?"

She replied, "Yes, your Honor," and then she proceeded by saying, "Your Honor, the State calls its first witness, Miss Anni Thompson."

Anni stood up. She was wearing a winter white dress of conservative length with gold buttons and white patent leather strapped sandals. Her auburn hair gently laid on her shoulders, covering part of the dress. Her wide, green eyes seemed to be a little glassy, and she portrayed a delicate gazelle who was chased for a mile and now was looking back to see if her pursuer was still following.

She stood at the witness box and the Bailiff instructed her to please put her left hand on the Bible and raise her right. She obeyed. Then the Bailiff asked Anni, "Do you swear to tell the truth and nothing but the truth, so help you God?"

Anni replied, "I do."

Then the Bailiff said "Please state your full name and address?" She did.

Then the Judge, with a friendly smile, told her to be seated. Turning toward the already half-way approaching D.A., Miss Slater, he said, "Please proceed."

The D.A. looked at Anni and said, "Hello, Anni. May I call you Anni?" Anni said, "Yes."

Then she asked, "How are you?"

Anni replied, "Nervous."

The D.A. said, "Don't worry, it's normal to be nervous. But really, there's only one person who should be nervous in this courtroom, the defendant."

Mr. Bentley jumped from his seat, "Your Honor, I object, the District Attorney is trying to influence the jury by her innuendos."

The Judge agreed, and warned Miss Slater to practice her trade by the book, otherwise he would cite her.

"I apologize, your Honor," was the answer from Miss Slater. However, she did not pass up the chance to give a dirty look in the direction of Joe Cobb.

She walked back to her table, looked down at some papers, and then slowly walking toward Anni, she said, "All right, Anni, would you please tell the jury what happened on that Wednesday in July."

Anni told her story from that day on, all the way to the day of her sexual engagement with Joe Cobb, leaving nothing out. And surprisingly, she gave a very detailed description of all the dates and happenings as they occurred. A few times, she sobbed, and used the ready supplied tissues.

Every time, this happened, the Judge asked her if she is ready to continue, or if she would like to have a rest.

Anni wouldn't have it. Each time she answered the Judge, "I'm sorry, I want to continue."

Her uninterrupted testimony, with the exception of her drying her eyes with a tissue, took one and a half hours. As she was going on, some of the lady jurors placed their hands on different parts of their faces, and three out of five guys looked down, and visibly shook their heads.

Her testimony was heart-wrenching. It almost sounded as a well thought out plot for a horror movie. Even Anni was thinking silently, My God, is this when the saying comes true: tell them the truth, they will never believe it. Or maybe the other saying whereby the truth sounds more fictional than the lie.

The D.A.'s voice broke up Anni's doubtful thinking, as Miss Slater turned towards Mr. Bentley, saying, "Your witness."

Mr. Bentley stood up and also looked down at his notes, and he took what seemed to Anni a sixty minute pause, but it was really about ten seconds in reality.

He approached Anni and said, "Hello Anni, may I also call you Anni?"

Anni snapped back by saying, "You can call me Miss Thompson."

Mr. Bentley said, "I apologize, Miss Thompson. Or is that Mrs. Thompson?"

Anni got even madder, and she snapped back with even more venom, "No, it's Miss Thompson. I'm divorced."

In a split second, she knew that she made a mistake by being rude toward Mr. Bentley. But she figured that anybody who would defend an animal like Joe Cobb was also her enemy.

The D.A. stood up and objected to the proceeding by stating that, "Your Honor, Mr. Bentley is badgering and harassing the witness, and practices the same wrong approach that he was objecting to as I was conversing with my witness."

The Judge stopped the proceedings and called for a side-bar.

Nevertheless, the first round, right or wrong, went to Mr. Bentley, since his aim was to introduce to the jury that Anni was a divorced woman. And since Anni was the one who mentioned it, she left the door wide open for him to walk right through. His aim now would be to raise some more unpleasant questions toward that issue.

As the Judge turned to his seat, he said to Mr. Bentley, "Please continue."

Sure enough, his first question was, "So you're divorced?"

The D.A. jumped up again and objected by saying, "Your Honor, Anni Thompson's divorce has nothing to do with this case.

The Judge looked at Mr. Bentley, who right away answered, "Your Honor, I haven't asked Miss Thompson about her divorce. She volunteered information to me, and therefore I'm entitled to probe the issue further."

The Judge said to the D.A., "Overruled," but at the same time warned Mr. Bentley not to overstep his bounds, and go only as far with the issue as pertains to the case.

Mr. Bentley agreed and said, "Yes, your Honor." Then turning toward the witness, he asked her the question, "So you are divorced, correct?"

This time, Anni got smarter. She figured that she was way above her head with this guy, and sobbingly turned toward the Judge, telling him that she didn't feel good and would like to take a rest.

The Judge looked at the clock and calmly said, "By all means, Miss Thompson. It's almost four o'clock anyway, and I think we've heard enough for one day."

Then he instructed Anni to return to her seat. As soon as she sat down, the Judge turned toward the jury, repeated his legalese and excused them until next day, nine o'clock in the morning. After the jury left, the Judge asked both attorneys if there was any other business that has to be taken care of.

The D.A. replied, "Yes, your Honor. We have supplied your Honor with a complete witness list. However, Mr. Bentley stated that his supplied witness list is not one hundred percent complete. We'd like your Honor to order Mr. Bentley to supply to us the complete list before tomorrow morning's procedures."

The Judge said to Mr. Bentley, questioningly, "Well, Mr. Bentley?"

Bentley said, "Your Honor, you know that the case was rushed on us. As such, I could not have completed the witness list one hundred percent, since we're still in the process of interviewing some potential witnesses, and the only reason I agreed to this speedy trial was to clear Mr. Cobb's name as soon as possible."

The Judge got mad, but he controlled himself by saying, "Look, Mr. Bentley, you're a reputable and capable attorney, but don't try to impress me with your charm and coyness. I'm not the jury and, by the way, you have three days to furnish me with a complete witness list. All others after that time I will exclude." Then he asked, "Is there anything else?"

"No, your Honor," answered the attorneys in an almost choir-like fashion.

Then the Judge wished them goodnight, instructed them to be present and ready by nine the next day with their witnesses. Then he left his bench, disappearing beyond his chamber's door.

The attorneys and their helpers started to pack their numerous carton boxes and placed each of them on luggage-carrying rollers that one mostly only sees in airports.

Anni and Helen were waiting for the D.A. to finish, and walked out with her to the parking lot. They exchanged a few questions and answers, but the D.A. firmly said that she would like to see Anni and Helen no later than six-thirty, either in her office or at their house. It was agreed to meet at the office of the D.A.

As Anni and Helen arrived at the D.A.'s office, they right away asked Miss Slater for a copy of both witness lists, Miss Slater's and Mr. Bentley's. The D.A. made the necessary copies and handed them over to both of them.

Miss Slater's witness' list seemed to be minuscule compared to the yet unfinished list of the defense, as Mr. Bentley mentioned during the trial. And Anni and Helen both remarked on it.

The D.A. smiled and said, "Ladies, the case isn't based on numbers, but on the cold facts. By the way, the reason I've called this emergency meeting is because I won't let Mr. Bentley chop you up as he started to do today, and almost succeeded.

"So hear me out," continued the D.A., and listen carefully. I don't want this relatively strong case to turn into a piss fight. Mr. Bentley started right away with his implications to confuse the jury by taking their attention away from the real issue, and trying to focus them on the divorce issue today.

"Tomorrow morning, before we start the proceedings, I'll visit with the Judge in his chambers in the presence of Mr. Bailey. We'll clear up a few things, including this newly raised bull about your divorce.

One thing, however, I strongly warn you about -- please do not volunteer any information that you weren't asked for, and answer only the questions that you were asked. Nothing else.

"If you know the answer, then give it with a short and positive tone. If you don't, then say that you don't know, or don't remember. But don't try to speculate and try to fix your case in your favor. That's my job. And if I think the questions are too harsh or too misleading or leading, I'll object. That's also my job.

"So wait until he asks you the question. Count to three, and then answer it calmly, with an absolutely relaxed tone. His aim is partially to upset you. If you count to three each time, it'll also give me the opportunity to object before you answer. That way you can cut out a lot of problems before they occur. Do you understand me, Anni?" she asked.

Anni said, "Yes."

"And do you agree with me, Anni?" she asked again.

Anni said, "Yes, and I am sorry if I caused any problems for you today. But the guy made me so mad when he started questioning me."

"You know," said the D.A., "this is exactly what I mean. This can't happen again. If it does, you're running the risk of damaging an otherwise strong case."

Anni and Helen were listening very attentively to every word the D.A. told them and, after agreeing, they hugged each other saying goodbye, and see you tomorrow. They left the D.A.'s office.

Chapter XIV

Anni arrived home from the D.A.'s office and was still a little bit upset from the experience that was involuntarily forced on her, and excused herself by going into her room and closing the door.

It was about nine p.m. and the room was pretty dark with only the shine of the full moon peeking through the unshaded window, and the gently waving branches of the old oak tree that was closely planted near the house.

She sat there quietly, just meditating, and suddenly she placed her hands together and started to pray. "My Lord, my God, please listen to my plea. Have mercy on me, and help me at my flight."

A tone inside her gave her the following answer: There is a greater power than you in existence. If you connect yourself to this higher power, than you and what you will experience are the origin and the gift of the life force that was given to you, and to all, as a birthright to be practiced all of your lives.

Anni broke down crying, but at the same time also thanked her Creator for giving her the unexpected grace in the form of an inner voice answer.

Her sobbing was overheard, and Helen knocked on the door, asking if Anni was all right.

Anni cracked the door open and answered Helen by saying, "I've never felt better in my life."

Helen said drastically: "Bullshit, then why are your eyes full of tears?"

"They're happy tears," Anni replied, "I've just talked to the best attorney in this and the next world."

Helen asked, "What in the world are you talking about?"

Anni told Helen her past half an hour experience, and even though Helen was not what one would call the most devout religious person, she remarked, "God bless you, and I hope everything will turn out for the best." Then Helen added to her sentence the following twisted quotation: "No matter how the saying goes, if you are loved and you love back, you can go home again."

This put a gentle smile on Anni's face, and she hugged Helen, saying, "Thank you, thank you very much."

One more hug, and then Helen said "We have a big day ahead of us, and we're both tired. So let us go to bed."

Anni retired to her room, but the experience of the previous meditation acted like a whirlwind in her head.

She started to think about her entire past life, which resulted in keeping the sand man away, and to close her eyes for a well-deserved sleep.

She recalled the stable, warm and loving environment that her parents, Joe and Renay had supplied her with as she was growing up.

The wishful thinking of wanting to go back to that era in her life, put a gentle smile on her face. She figured that then she could change the things that now afflicted her. She also started reminiscing about her marriage to John, and the happy years of their union before John strayed from his vows.

She silently questioned herself as to whether she was, or wasn't, at fault for John's betrayal. And how it could have been if not for both of them being so busy with their careers, and neglecting to nourish the most important mental object: their relationship.

In the shape of a self-confession, Anni thought that in the rat race of our time, how often we forget that our ambitions, and wanting to succeed in business, sidelines the most important thing -- what we are doing it for, or should be doing it for: sharing, loving, trust and respect from our mate.

Then her by now exhausted mind, reflected on her daughter Erica, and how she conceived her, through a strange man's semen, from a gene pool.

Her tired and, by now, melancholy mind wondered, what kind of man is Erica's biological father? Is he still alive? If she wanted to meet him? If she would like Erica to meet him?

Then the sand man completed his task and Anni fell asleep.

Chapter XV

The next day, Tuesday morning, as Anni and Helen arrived at the courthouse they had to go through the same barrage as the previous day. They fought themselves through the many reporters, and took the elevator to the courtroom.

The clock said 8:45 a.m., and everybody was there already.

Joe Cobb tried to catch Anni's eyes with a smirking face, but Anni knew this and avoided the incident by just looking toward the Judge's seat, staring with an unblinking eye.

The same could not be said for Helen, as she noticed Cobb's attempt, and stuck her tongue out at him.

The Bailiff called the mob to order at 9:15 a.m. and performed his well-practiced duty. Again, the jury was seated, the Judge walked in, and went through his usual rigmarole. Then he turned towards both attorneys and asked, "Are we ready to proceed?"

They both answered that they were.

The Judge called Anni back to the witness stand and reminded her that she was still under oath. Then he raised his hands toward Mr. Bentley and said, "Please proceed."

The defense attorney this time walked straight to the jury, said good morning to them, and quickly turned around to face Anni.

"Good morning, Mrs. Thompson," and he repeated himself again, "It is Mrs. Thompson, correct?"

Anni counted to three, and answered with a clear but cold voice. "No sir, you're not."

"What do you mean?" asked the attorney, "Is that not what you told me yesterday?"

After three, Anni said, "No sir, it is not what I told you yesterday."

Then the attorney smilingly said to Anni, "Okay, please tell me in your own words what you had said."

One, two, three ... Anni answered, "I said Miss Thompson."

The jury smiled, and the crowd became a touch noisy also, but they all stopped this time fairly quickly before the Judge could reach for his gavel.

"I am sorry, Miss Thompson," said the attorney, "I apologize, you're right. You told me yesterday that you changed your name to Miss Thompson after your divorce from Mr. Thompson."

There it was again, this finessed attorney, reversed the time right back to yesterday where he left off by reminding the jury that they were dealing with a 39-year-old divorced woman for a plaintiff.

Then he asked the next question, "Was this your one and only marriage?"

The D.A. again jumped from her seat with a loud objection, "Your Honor, Mr. Bentley has mixed up this criminal proceedings with divorce court. What has Miss Thompson's previous marriages to do with the charge that we have brought against Mr. Cobb?"

The Judge looked at the defense attorney and said, "Well, Mr. Bentley?"

The attorney said, "Your Honor, we're dealing with a very serious charge and the D.A. has asked for the maximum penalty. This case is based mostly on credibility issue, and therefore I have every right to probe into Miss Thompson's character and history. I owe this to my client and to the jury."

The Judge looked down for a second. And then, looking up at Miss Slater, said, "Your objection is overruled. However," he said to Mr. Bentley, "if I feel that you're starting a fishing expedition, I'll stop you very quickly."

"Yes, your Honor," he answered, and said, "Thank you."

Then he returned to Anni again and said, "Please answer the question."

Anni said, "I'm sorry, what was the question?"

The cross-examining attorney put a smile on his face and said, "All right Miss Thompson. The question was if this marriage to Mr. Thompson was your one and only marriage?" He paused, looking at Anni. This gave Anni the three seconds that they agreed on the previous night, and she answered, "Yes, yes sir. That was the one and only time that I was married."

"Okay, Miss Thompson, would you please tell the court the reason Mr. Thompson divorced you."

Again, the D.A. rose with a strong objection. "Your Honor, the counsel is leading the witness by assuming that Mr. Thompson divorced Miss Thompson."

This smart objection also gave Anni the clue to her answer.

The Judge said that the objection was sustained. "Please Mr. Bentley, re-phrase your question."

The guy was a smart cookie. He already got his answer to the question. Besides, he would never ask any question without knowing the answer to it ahead of time. And he avoided the ones not favorable to his case. He changed his line of questioning. "Miss Thompson, would you please tell me and the court if on that Wednesday in July that you claim you were raped, you had seen the perpetrator's face?"

"No, sir," Anni answered.

"Okay," he said. "Did you see his hands?"

"No sir," Anni said. "He had gloves on."

"Okay, Miss Thompson, can you describe the gloves."

"No sir," she said, "It was the furthest thing from my mind."

"Okay," said the attorney. "Then what was on your mind?"

"Deadly fear," answered Anni.

"Okay," said the attorney, "What else can you tell us about this perpetrator?"

Anni paused for a while and the D.A. stood up again, objecting.

"Your Honor, the counsel is trying to confuse the witness. If he wants to know a specific answer, then let him ask a specific question. But to ask Miss Thompson to deliberate as to what is possible, resembles a fishing expedition, and your Honor has warned him about it already."

"Okay," the Judge said. "Sustained. Please Mr. Bentley, I'm warning you the second time, no fishing expedition. Ask your next question."

The attorney said, "I'm sorry your Honor," and then went on with his next question. "Miss Thompson, did you see his shoes?"

"No sir," she said.

"Okay, did you see his hair?"

"No sir, he was wearing a mask."

"Oh, all right, then did you see his eyes?"

"No sir, he attacked me from behind."

"Okay, Miss Thompson, did you see the knife that he attacked you with?"

"No sir."

"Okay, Miss Thompson. In other words, you're telling us that you have nothing specific that you can recall observing of this so-called perpetrator?"

The D.A. jumped up again, and this time vigorously objected by saying, "Your Honor, there he goes again, putting words in the witness' mouth by testifying for her that she cannot recall anything specific about this animal. And furthermore, the counsel's testifying for his client by calling the rapist a so-called perpetrator."

"Okay, Miss Slater, your objections are definitely sustained, and I'm warning you again Mr. Bentley to stop your shenanigans. Otherwise, I'll impose a fine on you the next time."

Bentley apologized to the Judge. But it didn't matter because the jury had heard it, which was his intention.

At the same time, the Judge said, "It's ten-thirty, and I'm calling for a ten minute recess."

After the recess and the usual legal exercise, the session started again.

"Okay, Mr. Bentley," said the Judge. "At your leisure."

He answered, "I have no question at this time, your Honor, but I reserve the right to call back the witness, if it's needed."

"Granted," said the Judge. Facing Miss Slater, he asked, "Re-direct, Miss Slater?"

"Yes, your Honor," she said, "Just a couple of things to clear up, some of the mess that Mr. Bentley created."

"This made the defense attorney very mad. Standing up, he said, "Your Honor, I object to Miss Slater's un-called for remark. And if it pleases the court, please advise the D.A. to leave her childish judgment for her lady friends at coffee klatch time."

Now the Judge jumped up and only said. "Side-bar."

Returning, the Judge said, "The objection is sustained, and this time I'm warning you Miss Slater to curb your cynical remarks for your silent reservation, and stick with the issues at hand."

"I'm sorry," she replied, and the Judge signalled her to go on.

Approaching the witness, she began, "Anni, please tell me and the court if you have observed or not, one specific part of the perpetrator?"

"Yes, ma'am," she answered.

"And what was that?" asked the D.A.

Anni said that when he took out his penis, she noticed the abnormal size of it.

"Thank you," said the D.A. "Your witness, Mr. Bentley."

The defense attorney stood up, but this time he did not leave his place at the table. He just raised the following question, "Miss Thompson, are you a penis expert?"

Part of the courtroom, including some of the jury, broke out in loud laughter, and even the Judge couldn't bite away a small smirk from his face.

Only Anni, Helen, and the D.A. kept on a stern face and an indignant look.

The Judge kept banging with his gavel loud and numerous times, "Order in the court. Order in the court. If you don't calm down, I'll order the Bailiffs to empty the courtroom.

This time, they did not calm down as fast as the first time, and the Judge had to repeat himself one more time. "Order."

Then slowly the crowd returned to their human behavior and were silent.

The D.A. stood up and, looking at the Judge and then Mr. Bentley, in a monotone voice said, "Your Honor, I object to the counselor's drastic and obviously cynical remark, and if it pleases the court, I'm applying to the court to fine Mr. Bentley with a stiff penalty, since he's completely out of line -- not to mention unethical and rude. He hasn't found a decent way to question the witness, as he's supposed to be so well known for. I'm sure that the court agrees with me that he has crossed the line, and insulted the witness. I don't believe that in all my years of practice have I ever seen this kind of a cross-examination and, in particular, I am referring to the counselor's last inappropriate and vulgar insulting question." She kept standing.

The Judge said, "Mr. Bentley?" He stood up and made the following speech on his behalf.

"Your Honor, I do not see anything wrong or vulgar, not to mention insulting, with my question. Miss Thompson offered her testimony in the form of describing the perpetrator's anatomy as an abnormal size of penis. I have every right on my client's behalf to defend him with all my knowledge of the law. In my mind, I have every right to ask any witness on the stand if she or he is an expert in the field of the particular description the witness testifies to."

"Okay," the Judge said, and the sadness showed on his face, but he knew he had to rule in favor of Mr. Bentley. So he said, "The objection is overruled and I want to see both of you with a court reporter at the side-bar."

When they returned, the Judge called for the usual lunch break and told all concerned to return at two p.m., since the time had overrun to 12:30.

The prosecutor and her entourage went to the same eatery as the previous day, and this time they didn't have to worry about getting the same table, since the D.A. planned ahead by reserving it.

After they sat down and ordered, the D.A. turned towards Anni, touched her hand, and said, "You were great, Anni, don't worry about the penis incident. It couldn't have been avoided."

"That is one of our proofs that the case is built on, and please, bear with the embarrassment of that line of questioning, because it's absolutely necessary."

"By the way, I knew it was coming, and I wanted it to come. But I let Mr. Bentley introduce it. Believe me, he made a big mistake by doing it. The only reason I have objected is that I wanted to impress the jury by establishing some balance that I thought we slightly surrendered on a couple of previous occasions."

Anni said, "I have no problem with it, and the only two occasions that I had the problem were when he raped me."

"That's my girl," said the D.A. "You're going to be all right."

And, so to speak, they mini-celebrated as they all ordered sundaes for desert.

Again, the D.A. alerted the ladies that it was time to return to the court.

After the usual formalities, the proceedings resumed at 2:15 p.m. The Judge again signalled to Mr. Bentley and said, "Please proceed with your re-cross."

The attorney again just stood up and remained at his table.

"Miss Thompson, I'm sincerely sorry if you felt that I've insulted you. But as you heard, the Judge overruled Miss Slater's objection, and therefore, in the best interest of my client, I'm forced to ask you some not too comfortable questions. You have to answer them unless the Judge instructs you not to."

"I understand," answered Anni.

"Okay," he said. "Where were we?" After a couple of seconds pause, he said, "Oh yes, that's right, I was asking you if you were an expert in the field of men's anatomy, remember?"

Anni said, "Yes sir."

"So please, tell the court how many sexual partners you had prior to that Wednesday in July?"

Again, the D.A. stood up and objected to the fact that Miss Thompson was not on trial and that her prior amount of sexual partner or partners had nothing to do with the issue at hand.

"Your response, Mr. Bentley" said the Judge.

"Your Honor," Bentley answered. "I have every right to question the witness as to the number of her sexual partners in order to establish whether or not Miss Thompson is an experienced expert in the field of male genital anatomy."

Again a slight laughter was heard from the public, and the Judge firmly reminded them to be orderly.

"Okay, Mr. Bentley, the objection of Miss Slater is overruled. Please continue."

"Okay, Miss Thompson," said the attorney. "Please answer the question. By the way, do you remember the question, or would you like me to repeat it?"

"No, that won't be necessary, Mr. Bentley." For the first time, Anni said the defense attorney's full name. "I remember the question. Besides my husband, I had one previous partner, on one occasion prior to my marriage. And then the one unfortunate one with Mr. Cobb, one and a half years after my divorce from Mr. Thompson."

The courtroom was very attentive listening to Anni's answer. When she finished for a few seconds, it was so quiet in the courtroom that one could hear the traffic way down passing by.

The people and the jurors' faces were transformed to almost sorry looking peers toward Anni.

The quiet was interrupted by Mr. Bentley with his snapping voice. "Well, Miss Thompson, now what makes you an expert on the male's anatomy?"

Anni counted to three, then with a very solid voice, said, "Mr. Bentley, you don't have to have tuberculosis to know about tuberculosis."

This time some of the public started to applaud.

The Judge again quieted them and asked whether or not Anni was finished with her answer.

"No, your Honor," she said. "And please ask Mr. Bentley to wait this time until I've finished my answer. And don't let him interrupt me."

"Go ahead, Miss Thompson. I reassure you it won't happen," said the Judge. "I would charge him with contempt. Did you hear me, Mr. Bentley?"

He answered, "Certainly, your Honor."

"Proceed Miss Thompson," said the Judge, encouragingly.

Anni opened up by looking at the jury straight in the face.

"I have a B.A. from Harvard University for Science and Technology. My exhaustive studies and the professional field that I'm employed in since receiving my Diploma involves mostly the art of bio-technology and the entire anatomy of the human species, including the embryo and its complete function from fertilization to birth. I'm also a well-respected expert in the field of the female's and the male's function regarding sexual and bio-complex performance, and my provable credits also include the study of blood flow in the entire human body, including the penis and how it increases the size and the firmness of it. My studies have included the normality and the average penis as to the length and its diameter, plus at every age of the male's erection degree."

The hush went through the entire courtroom, and it took the Judge a few seconds to return from the mesmerized world that Anni had so eloquently created.

"Well, Mr. Bentley, please ask your next question," said the Judge.

"Thank you, your Honor. I have no further questions at this time, but I reserve the right to re-call the witnesses." He sat down.

"Miss Slater," said the Judge.

"Yes, sir. Yes, your Honor, I have a few questions. But before I proceed I'd like to ask the court to declare Miss Thompson to be an expert for the afore-testified field of science and technology."

"Mr. Bentley?" asked the Judge.

"No objection, your Honor," he said.

Then the Judge turned toward the jury and explained what it meant to be an expert, and what the jury's duty was in regards to the truth or the opinion of an expert.

It was 4:30 and the Judge called the proceedings to a halt until nine the next morning.

Chapter XVI

It was a cloudy Tuesday as the three ladies walked out of the court. But looking at their faces, you could've sworn that there was a brilliant sunshine since this day's victory had belonged to them. The D.A. said to Anni and Helen, "I feel like buying you guys a drink."

Anni answered, "I need one." They were laughing and walked to the nearby famous watering hole where practically the entire city's judicial personnel takes in its fix.

Next morning, 9:15 a.m. sharp, Anni Thompson, the now declared expert besides being the plaintiff, was back in the witness box.

The D.A., with a yellow notepad in hand, approached the Judge's bench and opened up with the following statement.

"Your Honor, I only have two questions left for the moment for my star witness, Miss Thompson."

"Proceed," said the Judge.

"Good morning, Miss Thompson," said the D.A. "How are you this morning?"

Anni answered, "Thank you. Much better than I was Monday, and definitely better since yesterday."

"Thank you," said the D.A.

"My second question for you is a more important one. Now that you've been declared and accepted as an expert by this court in the field of science and technology including, but not exclusively, the studies that you have testified to yesterday, do you still remain by the conviction that the male who committed that awful crime against you is in this courtroom?"

"Yes," Anni said, with an unshakable conviction.

The D.A. asked Anni if she could point out that male.

Anni rose from her chair, stood up with a perfectly straight body, turned slightly toward the defendant's table, raised her hand with an outstretched index finger, and pointed to Mr. Joe Cobb.

With a definite and very clear voice, she pronounced: "There is he, the beast that calls himself a human. Who on that Wednesday in July brutally raped me."

"Thank you, Miss Thompson. Please sit down," said the D.A.

Looking at the Judge and then the jury, the D.A. stated, "Ladies and gentlemen, please note that the plaintiff and expert has pointed out Mr. Joe Cobb as the male perpetrator who on that Wednesday in July kidnapped her, raped her, and against her will, maliciously and with forethought, performed sexual misconduct to her body.

"Thank you, your Honor, this is all I have for the moment from Miss Thompson. Mr. Bentley, it's your witness if you care to re-cross," said the D.A.

Miss Slater was a very competent attorney and regarded as one of the best D.A.'s in the country. She very seldom made a mistake while practicing her trade, but she made one this time. She recognized it right away by the opening next statement of Mr. Bentley to the Judge.

"Your Honor, now that the court has declared Miss Anni Thompson to be an expert, we've created the greatest conflict of interest that I have ever witnessed in my entire life practicing law."

Miss Slater knew it.

The Judge broke up the proceedings and signalled both attorneys to the side-bar.

As they returned after some five to ten minutes, the Judge turned toward the jury and made the following short, but physically recognizable, painful, speech.

"Ladies and gentlemen, I'll have to excuse all of you for a while since some very important legal matter has to be untangled between the attorneys and the court. I assure you that we will work very diligently and speedily in your absence, and let you return as soon as the matter's been resolved. Thank you."

With that, the Bailiff escorted the jury out.

It took the rest of the day to legally resolve the matter.

The next morning, after the jury was seated the Judge, with down-pointed head, walked in the courtroom, greeted the jury, and made the following explanation to them.

"Ladies and gentlemen, the court yesterday was working very hard all day to resolve a very important legal matter. After deliberation, the court informs you that a major legal mistake from Miss Slater, Mr. Bentley, and myself was allowed to enter in my courtroom and on the records. After clearing up the matter between the three of us, I made an application to the two participating attorneys and to the court to disqualify myself from the remaining procedure of this case. The two attorneys and my superiors have refused my application, and instructed me to continue with the trial.

"Therefore, the following agreed resolve will be entered in the records book. The proposal of Miss Slater and the acceptance of Mr. Bentley, including the declaration of this court accepting Miss Anni Thompson as an expert witness in her own interest, is a major conflict of interest.

"Therefore, let the records show that all testimony from Miss Anni Thompson regarding her knowledge and credentials as an expert witness is stricken from the records, and the jury is instructed to disregard all that they've heard on that matter. Thank you ladies and gentlemen."

A loud buzz filled the courtroom, and many reporters and T.V. newsmen left the room to rush to the phones, as the Judge called for a ten minute recess.

After the recess, Anni was called back to the witness stand.

The Judge asked Mr. Bentley if he would like to continue

with his re-cross. He said, no, but reserved the right to recall the witness if he felt it necessary. Miss Slater's answer was practically the same.

The Judge turned to Anni and said, "Thank you, Miss Thompson, you may step down.

"Miss Slater, please call your next witness," said the Judge.

The D.A. knew that she has to do some damage control, and so she started to call the character witnesses. The first one was Helen.

The D.A. didn't think that Helen's testimony helped tremendously for Anni, but no question, it did a lot of damage to Joe Cobb's character, and the mad looks that Cobb gave her and the steady movement in his chair proved that he was very uncomfortable as Helen's sometimes humorous, sometimes serious testimony made him look like a jerk and a loser. Cobb just shook his head up and down, giving the unspoken words, I will take care of you.

After Miss Slater finished with all her character witnesses, everybody -- including Anni's ex-husband, her employer, and some colleagues -- she knew that her strong suit lay in the D.N.A. and physical evidence.

Chapter XVII

It was the next Monday morning, and the trial entered the second week in continuation.

Miss Slater called her first witness, the detectives; then the police nurse; followed by the hospital emergency lady doctor; and finally the ace in the hole.

This D.N.A. expert was retained from one of the well-respected laboratory, and after some formal questioning, he was declared as a top D.N.A. expert.

After establishing the credentials, Miss Slater went through all the scientific proof with the expert and established that the D.N.A. that was taken that Wednesday in July belonged to Mr. Cobb and Miss Thompson.

She turned the expert over to Mr. Bentley for cross, but his reply was, "No questions, your Honor."

Miss Slater became very suspicious. What did he have under his sleeve now? she wondered. Was I making another mistake? It's been said that it is sad if an attorney starts to doubt her own case.

She blocked it out of her mind, but she also knew that the rest of the physical evidence, including the preserved clothing of Anni's, would not yield stronger evidence than the D.N.A., and the lawyer did not even question that. There were no fingerprints found, and scrapings from under Anni's fingernails yielded no damaging evidence against Cobb, since Anni did not fight, but prayed to save her life.

The D.A. finished with her evidence late Friday and said to the Judge that the prosecution rested.

The Judge dismissed the jury with the usual warnings, and instructed them and all participants to return to continue at 8:45 a.m. the following Monday, for a continuation, whereby the defense would start their case.

It was a long and hard weekend for Anni, Helen, and the D.A. They all got together on Saturday at the D.A.'s Office to discuss, evaluate, and plan their further strategies for the upcoming case by the defense.

The what-if's, maybe's and probabilities were flying back and forth between the three of them, and it was late Saturday as Anni and Helen returned home.

They were too exhausted and decided to go out for dinner.

As Anni and Helen sat down in the restaurant, like pigeons on St. Marcos Square in Venice, the guests started to descend on them.

Anni and Helen had completely forgot that the entire proceedings were covered daily on a minute-by-minute basis on the T.V., and their faces were just as familiar to the folks as any famous actors' or actress'.

The head waiter tried to minimize the chaos, but was not very successful. Anni and Helen ordered the food to take out, and they went home to consume their bounty.

The next day, Sunday, on Anni's plea, they both went to the local church, but called first to make sure that the hour at which they attended, there would be no service. They wanted to avoid the crowd's gawking, and the possibility of being hassled again. They were successful.

As Anni looked up at the huge crucifix that was predominating and permanently fastened to the church's stone wall, she silently started to talk to it.

"My Lord, give me the strength and the wisdom to withstand my ordeal, and please punish my perpetrator."

As she arrived home, an almost eerie inner voice answered her with the following sentence: You should have prayed to me for forgiveness and not for condemnation.

Anni's entire body, all of a sudden, was covered with

goosebumps. She shook herself and confessed to Helen about the whole incident.

Helen looked at Anni and said, "What? Are you nuts? Now you're starting to talk to yourself? Don't get crazy on me like a schizo-maniac. Come back to your common sense and stop punishing yourself."

Anni looked down and said, "You're right. I'm making myself crazy with this trial. It's not enough what he did to me previously. He's trying to ruin my life even now. Will this ever end?"

"Sure it will," Helen replied, "As soon as the trial's is over and they fry the S.O.B.."

They went to bed early since tomorrow was the big day when the second half of the draining trial would begin.

Chapter XVIII

It was a windless, calm, sunny Monday morning. It was the beginning third week of the famous trial, and even the weather was saying, Don't fool yourself, this is the calm before the storm.

As Anni and Helen arrived at the by now familiar courtroom, everybody else was there already.

The Judge walked in and everybody was standing. He told the people, "Please be seated."

There was what seemed an amount of anticipation from the crowd. Everybody was seated, and a silence filled the room and was only broken up with the Judge's voice calling Mr. Bentley for the defense. "Mr. Bentley, are you ready?"

"Yes, your Honor," was the answer.

"Please proceed," instructed the Judge.

"Your Honor, the defense calls for their first witness, Mr. Joe Cobb."

The good looking Cobb stood up.

As he started to walk towards the witness box, the public started to boo.

The Judge, hitting the gavel once loudly, told the crowd that one more outburst and he would extract them from his courtroom.

The crowd calmed down and the Bailiff administered the oath to Joe Cobb. Then Cobb was told to sit down.

Mr. Bentley, who was famous for his delicate tip-toeing; also had the reputation of a performer resembling a neurosurgeon in his trade. He approached his client in the witness box, greeted the jury, and said, "Good morning, Mr. Cobb."

Joe Cobb's cocky answer was, "It sure is, Mr. Bentley, good morning."

"How are you?" he inquired.

"Marvelous," was the reply of Joe Cobb.

"How come, Mr. Cobb?" was Mr. Bentley's next question.

Joe Cobb answered, "Because now finally I can tell my side of the true story."

"Thank you, Mr. Cobb," said Mr. Bentley. "That is what we're here for."

The class and the strategy with the first few exchanges was established, without a doubt. Nobody knew what was to be the outcome of the proceedings, but one thing was certain: Mr. Bentley was going to defend his client vehemently, with all his knowledge, and, if necessary, with the hypnotic effects of his style.

"Mr. Cobb," he opened, "Did you on that Wednesday in July, or at any other time, kidnap, rape, or with malicious forethought, sexually assault the plaintiff, Miss Anni Thompson?"

Cobb's answer was short, but very positively pronounced, "No, sir, I have not."

"Your witness, Miss Slater," said Mr. Bentley.

The D.A. stood up, looked at Joe Cobb from her position, and then she looked at her notes on the table. The silence and waiting was choking. But then, slowly walking toward Cobb, she greeted the jury with a friendly smile, and then said, "Good morning, Mr. Cobb."

"Good morning," was his reply.

"How are you?" she asked.

"Fine," he said.

"Are you nervous?" she continued.

"No, not at all," Cobb said, "I have no reason to be. I'm more mad than anything else."

"Why is that, Mr. Cobb?" asked the D.A.

"Because of this prosecution of an innocent man -- me," was his answer.

"Well, Mr. Cobb, why don't we let the jury decide your innocence or guilt, and begin with my questioning you. Okay?" said the D.A.

"That's fine with me," was his semi-arrogant reply.

"So, Mr. Cobb, would you please tell me and this court where were you on that Wednesday in July, let's say, from eight a.m. until twelve midnight. Can you tell us?"

"I sure can," said Cobb.

"You mean to tell us that you remember the particular day, hour by hour, minute by minute?"

"Yes, I do," he said.

"How come?" was the next probing question from the D.A.

"Because it was a very successful practice day for the softball team that I'm coaching at the local high school," he said.

"Oh, really?" said the D.A., and then she asked, "At what time did the practice begin?"

"At ten a.m.," was his reply.

"And you were there at ten a.m.?"

"Yes, ma'am, I was," he said.

"And how long did the practice take?"

"Until two-thirty p.m.," he said.

"And what was the weather condition that day, Mr. Cobb?"

"As I remember, it was drizzly, and off and on there were a couple of short spritz. But my girls are tough, and a couple of drops of water don't bother them, or me," he said.

"And were you there the entire time, Mr. Cobb?"

"Yes, ma'am," was his reply.

"You didn't leave the practice for anything at any time?"

"Oh, yes ma'am. Now I remember, I went one time to the restroom, and the girls were doing so good at the practice that I had promised them McDonald's and went to pick it up."

"And where was the restroom that you went to, Mr. Cobb?"

"They're connected immediately to the field," he said.

"And where is the McDonald's that you went to pick up the food?"

"Oh, about three miles from the field," he answered.

"Are you talking about the McDonald's six blocks away from Miss Thompson's residence?"

"Yes, that was the only one close enough by," he said.

"And what time did you leave and arrive back at the field, Mr. Cobb?" she asked.

"Oh, I don't know. It must have been around lunch-time, and I was back in thirty minutes."

"Okay, Mr. Cobb. I'm going to ask you if you, on that Wednesday in July, or any other time, forethoughtly and maliciously kidnapped, raped, and performed sexual misconduct on Miss Anni Thompson?"

"No, ma'am, I have not," he said.

"Well then Mr. Cobb, you heard the D.N.A. expert. How do you explain your semen in Miss Thompson that day?"

Mr. Bentley jumped up. "Your Honor, I object. The D.A. calls for an opinion from my client." The objection was sustained. Every move Bentley made, he was trying to impress the jury.

The D.A. thought that this was not a character or personality contest, but at the same time did not underestimate Mr. Bentley's talent. So as the Judge sustained the objection, she stepped up to the defendant, and started to heat up the examination. She remembered from law school that attorneys are in the hurt---business.

She asked, "Mr. Cobb, do you own any ski masks?"

Before he could answer, Bentley rose again and, after objecting, made the following complaint to the Judge. "Your Honor, the D.A. tries to portray my client in front of the jury as a maniac who would dress up like a priest and tie up his victims with his rosary beads, your Honor."

"Now that you mention it, Mr. Bentley," said the D.A. Miss Slater was an adamant prosecutor. Her tactics proved that her knowledge was at the pinnacle of the law, but she silently thought that Mr. Cobb would have been stoned to death for his crime in ancient times. But this was not the ancient times, and she knew that she had challenged the Judge's patience. "The next thing that you're going to tell me is that Mr. Cobb rates a Number ten on the Richter Scale of innocence, Mr. Bentley. Besides I don't think that the court and myself has any patience or tolerance for your antics."

Bentley got mad, "How dare you denigrate my expertise in the law? I believe you were a student in one of my classes as a beginner, when I was teaching law, and I'm instructing my client, Mr. Cobb, not to answer the question."

"I was not, and would not want to be, in any shape or form in a class of yours, Mr. Bentley," said the D.A.

"Stop it, stop it!" said the Judge. Looking toward the jury, he said the following: "Ladies and gentlemen, I will excuse you for about fifteen minutes while I take care of some very important business that cannot wait. I'll recall you as soon as possible." With that, he gave the sign to the Bailiff, and he escorted the jury out.

After they left, the Judge looked at both Miss Slater and Mr. Bentley, and said, "I won't allow a cockfight in my courtroom. Your unprofessional conduct is a disgrace to the justice system, and you should be ashamed of yourself. In my court, you don't crap until I say squat. Is that understood, Mr. Bentley?"

"Yes sir," he replied.

"Yes, Miss Slater?" he asked.

"Yes sir," she answered.

"Mr. Bentley and Miss Slater, I fine you each one thousand dollars for gross misconduct, and if this should happen again, next time the fine will be five thousand dollars, and the third time, I'll hold you in contempt. Did I make myself clear?"

"Yes, sir," they both answered.

"Thank you," said the Judge, and called for lunch recess.

When the participants and the public returned after lunch, the atmosphere had changed in the courtroom. Everybody was quiet and anxiously waited for the trial to resume.

"Mr. Cobb, please take the witness stand. You're still under oath," said the Judge. "Miss Slater, at your pleasure."

"Your Honor," said Mr. Bentley, standing up, "You haven't ruled on my objection to the last question Miss Slater posed to my client."

"The objection is overruled," said the Judge, "So, Miss Slater, repeat the question."

Miss Slater said, "Mr. Cobb, do you own a ski mask?"

"No, ma'am," he said.

"Mr. Cobb, did you hear the D.N.A. expert's testimony that they found hair samples on Miss Thompson's clothing from that day that belong to you?"

"Yes, ma'am, I heard it."

"Well, can you explain to us at least how did that get on Miss Thompson's clothing that day."

Bentley jumped up again, "Your Honor, same objection. The D.A. repeatedly asks my client for his inexpert opinion."

"Objection sustained," said the Judge.

"No more questions at this time, your Honor, but I reserve the right to recall the witness if it becomes necessary," said the D.A. "Your witness, Mr. Bentley." She thought she had boxed in the defense attorney.

"Mr. Cobb," Bentley opened up, "How long have you known Miss Thompson?"

"Oh ... about three years."

"And from what time did the two of you become more than just acquaintances?"

"Since May."

"You mean two months before that awful Wednesday in July?"

"Yes, sir."

"And when was the first time that the two of you had physical, sexual contact?"

"The same month," was his reply.

"And how often after that first contact did the two of you have sex?"

"Twice a week on average," he said.

"And when was the last time before that Wednesday in July that the two of you had sex?"

"The night before on Tuesday."

As the episode was unfolding, it fascinated the crowd.

Bentley conducted his defense like Toscanini the maestro. It sounded perfectly tuned. He appeared to make love to his profession.

Bentley was invading the D.A.'s patience, and started to get into her head. But she fought the brain-washing by staying calm and cool. She figured that sooner or later the jury will recognize

Cobb as a hormonal athlete and a psycho. For her, the whole question and answer session between Bentley and Cobb was a controlled violence.

"Okay, Mr. Cobb," said Bentley, "Do you own a ski mask?"

"No, sir, and I don't ski."

"Okay," said Bentley, "Please tell us about that whole day, Wednesday in July, what you did. When, where, and the timespan of everything. Please take your time, and nobody will interrupt you."

The D.A. thought: Wonderful, this is working out even better than she hoped. Let Cobb shoot himself in the foot, and she would just keep the rest of the facts in her envelope. She'd whip him into shape later. She also knew that Bentley was an ego-maniacal producer, and surprise was the signature of his trade.

He perfected his profession, like the art of dance. He acted like a polishing rag, gathering the remaining lint.

Miss Slater respected Bentley for his knowledge of the law, yet at the same time despised him for the tactics he used, even though they were admittedly successful.

The semi-softened ground suddenly turned to a frozen arctic tundra, between Bentley and Miss Slater.

The D.A. tried to get into Bentley's head, but he seemed to have a back-up plan for every situation.

This was one of the reasons why he was regarded as one of the top defense attorneys in the country.

The rage in Miss Slater's head, that Bentley created with his tactics, almost overpowered her common sense, but she disengaged the destructive thoughts.

People forgot the nation's budget problems, and the upcoming general elections were dwarfed by this case.

She admitted to herself, silently, that this genius, Bentley, practiced defense to perfection.

The D.A. felt that in her opinion Cobb should be castrated.

Mr. Bentley, with his inexhaustive mind, fought on like an immortal battalion.

"Go ahead, Mr. Cobb," said Mr. Bentley.

"Well," said Joe Cobb, "I've known Miss Thompson for

about three years, and about the first week of May, I asked her for a date. She said yes, and we met the next day.

She told me to come up to her condo for dinner. I went, and no more than a half an hour after dinner and chit-chat, we were sitting on a couch kissing. She started to feel me up, and like any red-blooded guy, I opened her blouse. She practically ripped my shirt off, and then she disrobed herself in front of me.

We made beautiful love that night, and a similar act repeated itself weekly. Until that Tuesday night when we had a fight."

"What was the fight about?" asked Bentley.

"She asked me to marry her," was his reply.

"And what was your answer, Mr. Cobb?" asked the attorney.

"I told her that marriage wasn't in my plan as far as she was concerned."

"And then what happened?" asked Bentley.

"She went nuts. She turned on me like an animal, and said something like, you S.O.B., I'm good enough to lay, but not for marriage. Then she told me to get my stuff and get out."

"And did you, Mr. Cobb?" asked Bentley.

"Of course, I did," said Cobb. I didn't hear from her for weeks until one day she showed up on the practice field with Erica."

"And what happened on that day, Mr. Cobb?" Bentley asked.

"She apologized to me and asked if we could start over, and she wouldn't mention the word marriage to me anymore."

"And what happened after?" probed the attorney.

"We made up and started to go out publicly," said Cobb.

"Did you have sex with Miss Thompson after you made up?"

"Of course," said Cobb. "But then one night after a wedding party, she invited me back to the condo and we made love. After love-making, she started to talk about marriage again. I think the wedding ceremony of my niece affected her."

"And then, what happened?" asked Bentley.

"I told her no and we started to argue again. She told me this is it -- she didn't want to see me again, and told me to get out."

"And did you, Mr. Cobb?"

"Yes, of course. And the next thing I knew, two detectives came to my house and arrested me. You know the rest."

"Okay, Mr. Cobb," said the attorney; "What about your trip to McDonald's that Wednesday in July?"

"Well, like I told the D.A., I got into my car about lunchtime and went to the McDonald's to get a large order for the girls. I was even joking with the girls at McDonald's.

They all know me since I go there often with my girl's softball team."

"Okay, Mr. Cobb, what about your hair on Miss Thompson's clothing?"

"My God, answered Cobb, my hair must be all over that condo. I don't know how she got it on her housedress."

"Thank you, Mr. Cobb. Your witness, Miss Slater."

The Judge stopped the proceeding and said, "Ladies and gentlemen, it's late so I'm calling for a recess. I'll see you all back tomorrow mornirg at 8:45.

Chapter XIX

It is Tuesday morning and the third week of the trial of Anni Thompson and Joe Cobb. And as the adversaries, the jury, and the public, were standing and waiting for the Judge, Anni felt that as if something would be decided today, like it could not be avoided.

How sixteen days could transfer a perfectly normal, beautiful, 39-year-old healthy woman to become phobic, was even to Anni now, staggering.

"Mr. Cobb, please take the witness stand. You are still under oath," said the Judge. "Miss Slater, at your pleasure."

"Thank you, your Honor," was her response. She greeted the jury, then Mr. Cobb, and asked him, "Mr. Cobb, you were telling us that you went to pick up the food from McDonald's on that Wednesday, correct?"

"That's correct, ma'am," he answered.

"Did you phone in the order ahead of time, or did you place it on your arrival at McDonald's?"

"I don't remember, Miss Slater," was his answer.

"Okay, Mr. Cobb, you told us that you and Miss Thompson were seeing each other since May, right?"

"That's right," he said.

"Well, Mr. Cobb, can you tell us if anybody ever, on any occasion, saw the two of you together."

"No, ma'am, I can't. They might have or they might not have. Mostly I met Miss Thompson in her condo, or on the parking lot of the local shopping center, and we got busy in my car."

"Oh, I see," said the D.A., "you two, or either one of you, didn't want the public to know of the affair, right?"

"Not me, ma'am, it was Miss Thompson's idea."

"No more questions, your Honor, at this time. But I reserve the right to call Mr. Cobb if that should become necessary."

"So noted," said the Judge.

"Mr. Bentley," said the Judge, "Re-direct."

"No questions, your Honor."

After Cobb left the witness box, Bentley called countless character witnesses on behalf of his client, and before he was through, it was late Thursday morning. That week, one tabloid came out with the headline, "The Marriage Minded Divorcee."

Anni was taken apart twice by this rape artist, and now the reporters invaded her mind and soul. The pressure of insecurity was weighing on her mind and looks. She seemed to age six years in eighteen days. Her head was like a brewing volcano, ready to erupt.

Then, after lunch on that Thursday, Mr. Bentley called to the witness stand the famous D.N.A. expert, Mr. Pleck. After he was sworn in, Bentley greeted him, "Good afternoon, Mr. Pleck."

"Good afternoon, Mr. Bentley," he replied.

"Mr. Pleck, would you please tell the court your credentials and expertise."

He started to rattle off his education and employment, and it took fifteen minutes before his mouth finally came to a smirking halt.

"Thank you, Mr. Pleck," said Bentley, then continued, "Your Honor, I would like the court to declare Mr. Pleck an expert witness in the field of D.N.A.."

The whole courtroom once again started laughing.

"Order in the court," said the Judge, and then he instructed the jury accordingly about an expert witness. "Go ahead, Mr. Bentley," ordered the Judge.

"Mr. Pleck," asked Bentley, "have I instructed you to examine all the D.N.A. reports that I have obtained by court order, including Erica Thompson's from the hospital where she was treated at one time?"

"Yes, you have, Mr. Bentley."

"And whose D.N.A. reports have you examined?"

"Miss Anni Thompson's, Mr. Joe Cobb's, and Miss Erica Thompson's."

The D.A. flew from her chair. "Your Honor, I object. What has Miss Erica Thompson's D.N.A. have to do with this case?"

"Mr. Bentley?" asked the Judge.

"Your Honor, I beg the court's indulgence to bear with me, and I'll explain the reason shortly."

"Okay, Mr. Bentley," said the Judge, "The objection is overruled, but if I notice the slightest chance that you are again on one of your fishing expeditions, I'll stop you very quickly."

"Thank you, your Honor, said Bentley and continued. "Well now, Mr. Pleck, after you have examined all three of the aforementioned D.N.A.'s, what in particular came to your attention?"

"After careful examination, I have one hundred percent, beyond any shadow of a doubt, concluded that Erica Thompson is the biological offspring of Miss Anni Thompson and Mr. Joe Cobb."

Anni fainted, falling from her chair.

The proceedings were halted, and a ten minute recess was called by the Judge. The court nurse took care of Anni, and everybody returned to the courtroom.

The Judge asked Anni if she was ready to continue.

Anni sat there like a mannequin, but said, "I think so."

At the same time, her married life flashed in front of her.

Could it be possible, that destiny played such a cruel joke on her, that the semen donor, sixteen years ago, was the then college-attending Joe Cobb?

Did the new technology of D.N.A. punish her now for her and her ex-husband's decision to interfere with nature sixteen years ago, to under go in vitro fertilization?

Is this beast in the courtroom, Joe Cobb, the biological father of her daughter, Erica?

If the defense's D.N.A. expert is correct, then Joe Cobb must be, said her inner voice.

Yet somehow Anni was trying to refuse the truth, about the new revelation, and the most likely fact, made her nauseous.

Anni felt that this huge coincidence, however possible, would not change her mind about Joe Cobb. On the contrary, she felt nothing but contempt toward him.

The expert returned to the witness stand, and Mr. Bentley opened up with, "Your Honor, this morning we filed a Motion at the lower court for child custody, on behalf of Mr. Cobb for Erica Thompson."

And with that, he walked over to Anni. Reaching in his pocket, he pulled out the subpoena and served it on her.

It was late and the Judge called it a day until 8:45 Friday morning.

The same night, the D.A. got a phone call from Mr. Bentley. He offered a plea bargain.

He said, "We're willing to drop the child custody suit forever, if your client drops the rape charge."

"Not on your life," was the D.A.'s response, "But I'll inform Miss Thompson about your diseased proposal, since I am obligated to do so. However, I will advise her vigorously to turn it down."

"Let me know," was Bentley's answer, and he hung up.

The D.A. called Anni right away and told her about the offer.

Anni said, "No. I'll kill him first."

"Well," the D.A. said, "I wouldn't advise it. After all, he is the biological father of your daughter, if the expert is correct. And I am sure he's not bluffing.

However, I will instruct our D.N.A. expert to re-check his findings."

Miss Slater, before leaving her office, obtained the copies of the three D.N.A. tests and reports. She called her D.N.A. expert.

She explained the situation and that she had to be in the court the next day at 8:45 a.m.

The old friend and D.N.A. expert, said, "I'll do it. It will probably take two to three hours, but I'll do it. I'll pick up the test results and reports from you, and after I've examined them, I'll call you. Okay?" he asked.

"You're a doll," answered the D.A.

The call came at about eleven o'clock that night.

"The defense expert's correct, Miss Slater," said the D.N.A. expert. "Erica Thompson is, without a doubt, the offspring of Anni Thompson and Joe Cobb."

"Thank you," Slater said. "Thanks a million," and she hung up.

The next morning as the court proceedings started, Miss Slater called Joe Cobb back to the witness stand.

As he took the stand, he was reminded that he was still under oath.

Then Miss Slater asked him the first question. "Mr. Cobb, have you ever in your lifetime donated sperm?"

"Yes I have," was Cobb's answer.

"Where, and when?" was the next question from Miss Slater.

The answer came from Cobb, like daggers, fast, arrogant, but without any hesitation. He stated, that when he was attending college sixteen years ago, he needed money, and named the reputable clinic where he donated his sperm.

Miss Slater asked the judge for a five minute recess for the reason that she would like to talk to her client, Anni Thompson, in private to confirm certain new evidence.

The judge granted her request and Anni and Miss Slater proceeded to a private room in the courthouse.

"Anni," said Miss Slater, "I've only two questions to ask you. How did you become pregnant and where?"

Anni told Slater her story, including the in vitro procedure, and the clinic where it was performed.

Joe Cobb's testimony was correct: the time, and the name of the clinic coincided with Anni's confession to Miss Slater.

As Anni and Miss Slater returned to the courtroom, Cobb went back to the witness stand.

Miss Slater only said one long, but keen to the point, sentence. "Your honor, in regard to the new evidence the prosecution is faced with, I have no further questions for Mr. Cobb."

The judge excused Cobb from the witness stand.

Chapter XX

After some more insignificant witnesses, the trial had ended, on the fourth week, Wednesday, and was handed over to the jury for deliberation.

The newspaper had for its headline, "The Anni Thompson Saga." On the six o'clock nightly news, all T.V. channels reported first on the case.

The D.A. was satisfied that she handled all the key areas, including details, very thoroughly.

Mr. Bentley had walked out of the courtroom looking very cocky.

The offer came one more time in the courtroom from Mr. Bentley. "How about it, Miss Slater, do we make a deal?"

Anni was standing next to the D.A., and answered for her. "Get a grip on yourself. Tell that bastard client of your's to drop dead."

"You heard my client," said the D.A., and they all went home.

Anni looked strung out and Helen hugged her.

"Don't worry, honey," she said to Anni. "The bastards hours are numbered, and then he'll be somebody's wife in the prison."

The D.A. insisted to Anni, over the phone, not to come to the courthouse any more until she called her, when the jury tells the Judge that they have reached a unanimous verdict.

Thursday passed by. On Friday there was also no news from the jury.

Anni had her worst weekend, and phoned the D.A. Sunday night.

"What's going on? Why does the jury take this long?"

"They probably all went home to think it over during the weekend," said the D.A. on the phone. "Tomorrow they probably will reach a verdict. I'll call you. Rest." And with that, the D.A. hung up.

Monday passed by. Finally, Tuesday, the D.A. informed Anni that the jury agreed on the verdict, and Anni and Helen should come to the courthouse by 10:45 a.m. as the jury would be let back in the courtroom for the 11:00 a.m. rendition of the verdict.

Anni's heart jumped, and she told the D.A. that she and Helen would be there on time.

As they approached the courthouse, all the reporters once again bombarded them with the uncomfortable questions, and the countless cameras were flashing.

Anni and Helen, without answering to any one of them, fought their way into the courthouse, and then went up to that familiar courtroom.

Everybody was there already, and both of the attorneys were contemplating the unthinkable, but possible, outcome.

The Judge finally walked in as the Bailiff told the crowd to stop talking, and remain silent.

The Judge asked the Bailiff to please bring in the jury, that had remained the same seven women and five men from the beginning of the trial.

They walked in like the twelve apostles to their appointed chairs, and after they were seated, the Judge asked the forelady if they had reached a verdict.

The forelady said, "Yes, your Honor."

Then the Judge asked her if the verdict was unanimous.

The answer was yes again.

Then the Judge asked the two attorneys and their clients to please rise. The Judge turned towards the standing forelady and asked her the last, but most important question. "How does the jury find Mr. Joe Cobb, on all the counts, guilty or not guilty?"

The forelady, with a clear and distinctive voice, pronounced, "Not guilty, your Honor."

Most people were screaming and cursing, and Mr. Bentley and Joe Cobb hugged each other with a strong handshake.

The Judge for a few seconds tilted his head downwards, and Anni just stood there, silent and motionless.

The Judge hit his gavel, and everybody stopped.

The attorneys called each juror for their individual verdict, and they all said "Not guilty."

Then the Judge asked everybody to sit down, including the jury. He thanked the jury for their exhausting participation and then, turning toward Mr. Cobb, made the following short and painful speech.

"Mr. Joe Cobb, the court apologizes for the bother and inconvenience that it has caused for you. The jury found you not guilty. You are free to go." He hit one more time with his gavel, and declared the trial to be finished. He stood up, and walked back into his chambers.

Miss Slater thought how ironic is our justice system? If the jury finds the defendant guilty, the Judge has the power to set the verdict aside. But if the verdict is not guilty, his hands are tied like the hostage's hands.

And may be he is a hostage -- the hostage of our justice system, and the law that governs it.

Anni, Helen and Erica arrived home sobbing and broken-hearted, the disappointment visible on their faces.

Anni said to Helen and Erica that tomorrow morning, she was moving back to her condo with Erica.

They all laid down and did not get up until the next morning at six o'clock.

Anni and Erica kissed Helen, and thanked her for everything she had done for them, and the sacrifices that she so bravely endured.

Then mother and daughter left for the condo.

Chapter XXI

As Anni and Erica settled back into their condo, Erica said to her mother, "You know, maybe Joe wasn't the guy who raped you. Did you ever think about that?"

Anni started to raise her voice louder and louder. "How dare you even ask me such an insulting question!"

They argued loud and long and, at the end, Erica informed her mother that she is moving to her father's at the coast.

Anni said, "You might as well. It'll be better for everybody's sake to take time out."

Erica phoned her father, and the next morning she was on the plane to the coast.

The newspapers were splashing the not guilty verdict, and on television the news programs did the same.

On various talk shows, different spin doctors explained the whys and why-nots of the right or wrong verdict.

It became practically a cottage industry, as unexhausted for and against guest attorneys appeared nightly.

Even a few jurors were interviewed, and their decisions news-casted.

Some of the shows even had open eight hundred number calling lines.

The public responded greatly with their speculations with for or against opinions.

In one day, Joe Cobb went from grunge to glamour, and Anni Thompson from respect to ridicule.

Anni's employer called her as to when she thought she could return to her well needed job.

Anni asked them if they would still want her? The C.E.O. reassured her that he was not part of this masquerade, and some of the residual effects from the case would die down. In a couple of weeks, the public would be fed a new story, only to forget this one.

The next few days, anywhere Anni went -- from the food store to the gas station, in the coffee houses, to the mall -- she received mixed looks from the public. Some of the looks were interpreted by Anni to be accusatory.

Some young punks even asked her at the mall, "How about it, sweetie, let's go for a round."

Anni was a proud woman and the trial made her otherwise soft nature a lot harder. She kept her head up high, with a grin-and-bear-it smile on her face. She closed her eyes and mind to the dirty looks and remarks from all concerned, and never commented to anybody who approached her from far or close distance.

A week later, Erica called her with a crying voice. Her father, Mr. Thompson, had a major heart attack and had passed away.

Anni told Erica that she would be on the next available plane to her side. Then she informed Helen about the unfortunate history, and said, "I'll see you in about a week."

Anni called the airline, packed some necessary items, and the same day she was on the plane to Erica.

Mr. Thompson had remarried after his divorce from Anni, to a wealthy woman fifteen years older than him. This lady had a son named David Lang from her previous marriage.

David was a twenty-nine-year-old Yale graduate, and got his law degree from the University of Stanford. He was in his third year of successful private practice and he had a good reputation as a defense attorney in the criminal field.

As Anni exited the gate on her arrival, she was greeted by Erica and David. Anni and Erica hugged and kissed each other sobbingly, and then Erica introduced David to her mother.

As they arrived at this gorgeous villa of her ex-husband's, she was also introduced to Mr. Thompson's by-now widow.

Anni was going to make a sleeping arrangement at the hotel, but Haidy, the widow, would not hear of it. "Oh no," Haidy said. "You'll stay right here. After all, we're all family now."

Anni gave in and agreed to stay.

The funeral arrangements were made by Haidy and Erica, and after some explanation of what happened to Erica's father, they all went to their sleeping quarters exhausted.

The next day was the first day in the funeral home to view the remains of Mr. Thompson. The visitors who came to show their respect signed in the visitor's book, and that day it added up to 439.

Mr. Thompson and Miss Haidy Lang's family were very well known and respected on a wide scale at the coast. Many dignitaries attended the wake and the burial site.

After the funeral, a dinner was arranged for the close relatives at a well reputed hotel's main dining room. The party numbered sixty-two.

At about six p.m. as the Thompson's arrived home after the dinner, the housekeeper informed Anni that about fifteen minutes earlier, a gentleman had called long distance for her and left a number to call him back as soon as possible.

As Anni looked at the number, her heart almost stopped. She knew the number by heart. It was the detective's number from her city's police department.

She placed her wide rimmed black hat, pocketbook, and gloves on the nearby wardrobe table and asked the hostess, Haidy, if she could use the telephone.

Haidy answered, "Of course, this is your home for the duration of your stay. Please feel free as you would in your own home." And then she showed Anni to a more private side room that was the study of Mr. Thompson, and said, "You'll be more private in here." Haidy closed the door after Anni entered and re-joined Erica and David.

They were sitting in the living room, and after some light conversation, the peace was interrupted with the loud scream that came from the study. They all rushed to the door, and after knocking on it, Erica opened it.

Her mother was kneeling on the floor with her head in her hands, and the receiver of the phone was on the floor.

Erica rushed to her side and said, "What's the matter, mommy. What happened? Are you all right?"

She looked up with teary eyes to Erica, and made the following remark. "He killed her."

Erica inquired, "Killed who? What're you talking about?"

"Helen's dead," Anni replied.

Now Erica screamed, "Oh my God, no! What happened?"

Anni told Erica, that she was told by the detective the following: Helen was raped and her throat was slit right through the jugular.

Erica asked Anni immediately, "Do they know who did it?"

Anni said to the threesome -- Erica, Haidy and David -- that the only things the cops know is that a ski masked man was fleeing the scene, according to an eyewitness.

Anni re-composed herself and called the airlines. The next morning she was on the plane, accompanied by Erica, back to her condo.

She called the detective right away, and he came over the same afternoon. He informed Anni of all the details of Helen's rape and murder. He also said to Anni that they questioned Mr. Cobb, but he seemed to have a perfect alibi. There were no fingerprints found. Neither did they find any semen or foreign hair on Helen. The only clue they had was the eyewitness who saw a ski masked tall man running from Helen's house.

The detective informed Anni when the coroner would be finished with Helen's corpse, and when it would be delivered to the funeral home. Then he hugged Anni and said, "I"ll be in touch with you," and left.

The well published trial of Anni Thompson and Joe Cobb had also made the name Helen Richter a household name, and hundreds came to the funeral home, church, and cemetery to pay last respects to the unfortunate lady.

After Anni and Erica returned home, Erica said to her mother that the next day she would visit her ex-classmates before she returned, the day after, to the coast.

Anni just nodded, saying, "Okay."

Chapter XXII

The day after the funeral was the big day of championship game when Joe Cobb's team, the Tigers, faced their strongest competitors, the Braves. The stadium was full and only standing room was available for visitors who did not get their tickets ahead of time.

As the announcer introduced the visiting team, one by one, and then their coach, everybody was booing. And then finally, he started to announce the home team with their coach, Mr. Joe Cobb.

The public was applauding as a lady with a `kerchief covering her hair and huge sunglasses on her eyes entered the field from the standing room public.

She walked directly to the standing microphone at the pitcher's mound where Mr. Cobb was only a six foot distance away. She faced the microphone and everybody got silent, thinking that she would probably sing the National Anthem.

But instead, she had just said one short sentence. "This is for Helen!"

And with that, she pulled out a revolver from her dress pocket, and shot Joe Cobb dead center in the forehead.

Then she leaned over the fallen body of Joe Cobb and pumped one more bullet in his heart, saying, "I want to make sure nobody can get a heart transplant."

Everybody heard her short speech through the sensitive standing microphone.

Then she dropped the gun on the dead body of Joe Cobb. Facing the mic, she removed the kerchief from her hair, and the sunglasses, and made the following announcement: "Ladies and gentlemen of the jury, my name is Miss Anni Thompson, and I have just executed Mr. Joe Cobb for his beastly and animalistic crime against myself and Miss Helen Richter, and humanity."

Then she stepped aside, put her hands behind her back, and clutched them.

The dead silence was only broken with one loud scream from a young lady in the stands. It was Erica Thompson.

Then the whole public got loud as the security police, with the attending ambulance and first aid personnel, rushed to the field.

They cuffed Anni Thompson, and after examining the body of Joe Cobb, they bagged it.

Then four guys started to carry Joe Cobb's body on the stretcher toward the middle exit, and as Anni followed closely with the cops, it looked like a funeral procession.

As they got half-way to the exit, the crowd first slowly, and then loudly, started to applaud.

Anni was escorted to the city jail and, next morning, in front of the same Judge who presided at her trial, was arraigned and charged.

Anni had no defense attorney, and so the Judge asked her, "Miss Thompson, where is your attorney?"

"I don't need any," replied Anni.

He said, "Miss Thompson, this is a very serious charge that you are faced with."

Anni replied, "No, your Honor, I was faced with a lot more serious situation before. This is a small problem compared to that."

Nevertheless, the Judge appointed legal aid, and in five minutes, an attorney was standing next to Anni.

Then the Judge asked the inexperienced attorney, and Anni, if they would like to have a short conference, but Anni refused.

So the Judge said to Anni, "Miss Thompson, you're charged with first degree murder of Mr. Joe Cobb. How do you plead?"

"I am guilty of killing him, your Honor."

Then the Judge entered the plea, and set the trial date. He also denied bail and Anni was escorted back to jail.

Chapter XXIII

Erica visited her mother in jail, closed the condo, and returned to the coast to Haidy and David. She told the whole story, and David called Anni in jail to offer his services to her.

Anni asked David, "Why would you want to defend me, since I don't want any defense for my action?"

David had to do quite a bit of convincing, but Anni finally agreed to let David take over her case.

The detective went to the lady coroner's lab to look at Cobb's body before it was released to the relatives. Before he could ask the first question, another detective arrived at the Coroner's lab and asked the first one; "What happened to him?" pointing to Cobb's body.

"He got lead poisoned," the first detective answered. "What do you think happened to him? Anni Thompson saved humanity from this beast and shot him."

As the lady coroner was explaining to the detectives her findings, one of the detectives asked her about the penis size of Joe Cobb.

She started to laugh.

The detective asked her, "Why do you laugh?" "Because I only examine them when they are stiff," said the lady coroner.

And then she laughed again, and said, "Well, they're never this stiff when the owner still breathes."

Now, they were both laughing.

"Anyway," said the detective, "Talk to me."

She said, "It was abnormally huge, and a donkey would've been satisfied with it. By the way, the guy must have been severely horny, because it was ripped in a couple of small places."

"Oh my God," said the detective, "Please don't release the body. I'll have my D.N.A. expert take samples, and then you can throw him in the nearby sewer."

They parted laughingly, and the Coroner promised to retain the body of Cobb until further instructions.

Anni, in jail, was thinking, since she now had all the time in the world. The whole planning and killing of Joe Cobb was going through her head over and over again.

Anni was a lady who was against violence, her philosophy was that even that promiscuity was poison. But she lost it. Every nerve ending of her's was touched by this animal.

The law could not prove anything that connected this guy to the murder, but Anni knew it was so. So there was no remorse in her thinking. She had wanted revenge. She had wanted justice. And she was not sorry that she silenced Cobb once and for all.

After a few weeks, the detective received his D.N.A. expert's report, and finally, the D.N.A. was found from Helen Richter, in the crevices of Joe Cobb's penis.

He reported his findings to the D.A. and also told Anni's attorney, David, the good news.

When David visited and told Anni, she just answered very softly, "I always knew it, but nobody wanted to believe me.

God, forgive me for what I have done, but if the circumstances would repeat themselves, I would probably do the same."

David reassured Anni that their case improved just about one hundred percent.

"Not mine," Anni said. "My best friend in the world is dead because of me. He probably would never have hurt her if I hadn't involved her in my trial."

"You're right," said David, "But believe me, you and Helen weren't the first two women he's hurt. And in a way, thanks to you, he'll never hurt anybody again."

They talked over some more strategies, and said goodbye until the next meeting.

All concerned were getting feverishly ready for the upcoming trial of the murder case of Anni Thompson.

The D.A. interviewed everybody connected to the case concerning even the slightest details.

David did the same. First, he had to convince Anni that she should change her mind about her philosophy about shooting Cobb, and try to learn to cooperate with him, or they were like dead fish in the water.

David wanted to safeguard Anni, and he felt that he had the talent and ingredients, not to mention ability, to detour the jury, and provide some restoration to Anni's life. He was also grappling with the idea that if he could convince his client to plea bargain, the possible sentence could be a lot less jail time. All this was, of course, the solemn presumptuous thinking of David, since he did not mention his thoughts to Anni.

He figured it was too early to entertain the subject with Anni, or the D.A. However, David knew that this was a no-brainer and, sooner or later, the subject of plea-bargaining would surface.

On one occasion when David visited Anni in jail, Anni raised the question: "So what are you going to do at, or before the trial?"

David thought that maybe Anni had changed her mind and she was willing to talk about wheeler-dealing with the D.A., so he asked her, "You mean like plea bargaining?"

"I've never thought about that, but since you're mentioning it," said Anni, "What about it?"

"Well, I am certainly going to discuss it with the D.A. at the appropriate time," said David.

"And what if they turn you down," asked Anni.

"Well, there's really no plan for it yet," answered David, "But I think they'll most likely consider it. Anyway, it's too early, and too premature, to talk about it now."

Chapter XXIV

Finally, the trial date arrived.

When Anni had been in jail for three months prior to her trial, Erica had only visited once to show her mother her high school diploma, but she came with David to the trial.

The judge said, "Miss Anni Thompson, you are charged with the willful and forethought murder of Mr. Joe Cobb. How do you plead?"

David answered, "Not guilty, your Honor."

The second trial against Anni again was televised. The country had not seen so much excitement since her first trial. The pressure from the prosecution mounted as the trial got older.

David proposed a plea bargain, but was flatly refused.

As the witness for the prosecution, the detective was called to the stand. Shortly after, David started his cross-examination.

"So," he said, "when you were investigating the case, what in particular came to your attention?"

The detective answered that according to the State's D.N.A. expert, he found Helen Richter's D.N.A. in the penis crevices of the deceased, Mr. Joe Cobb.

The whole courtroom started to scream, and made loud remarks, but the Judge silenced them.

The D.A. stood up and objected right away.

"Your Honor, we're not trying the deceased, but his murder. Committed by Miss Thompson."

The Judge looked at David, and asked, "What about it?"

David answered, "Your Honor, the two cases are very closely related, since the accused killed the deceased for raping her, and the murder of Helen Richter."

The Judge sustained the D.A.'s objection, and explained to David, "That does not give the right -- even if that would be the proved case -- for your client to be a vigilante and take the law in her own hands. Therefore, the D.A. is right and the objection is sustained."

That was all right with David. The jury had heard it.

The trial went on for four weeks, and after the jury deliberated for six days, the verdict was guilty as charged.

The only option that was left for David after the verdict is to appeal to the jury for leniency at the sentencing and punishment phase of the case.

But Anni was sentenced to 25 years to life, with a minimum jail time of no less than 20 years.

David looked at Anni's sunken body in her chair. She looked physically devastated. David thought: No matter how strong one's heart, if the body falls apart under tremendous strain, the heart will die with it. He also tried to explain to Anni that sometimes in our justice system, we defy the common sense of handing out the appropriate punishment according to the crime that was committed.

Sometimes the law completely disregards the extenuating circumstances, and this was definitely a painful example of.

David went to the Appellate Court, but his appeal was rejected, and the sentence from the lower court was reconfirmed.

Anni said to David: "It was the wrath of God."

Anni was put on suicide watch, but after a while, when she showed no tendencies, the practice was discontinued.

Instead a terrific visitation was noticed on Anni's face. She was praying most of the time, and behaved as an outstanding prisoner. She became the prison librarian, and everybody loved and respected Anni, including the other inmates.

But Anni walked around in the prison with a frozen smile all the time, like a mannequin. Her dignity and grace was preserved, but something was missing from her individuality.

She agreed with everybody, and when David came to visit once every two to three months, he gave all different excuses to Anni why Erica didn't visit at all.

Anni just said calmly, "I understand. She's not proud to have a mother who's in jail for murder."

Into Anni's third year of jail time, on one visit, David told her that Erica and he got married, and that he had wanted to inform Anni, but Erica was against it.

Anni replied, "Oh, that's all right. I'm so happy for the both of you."

David was still very enthusiastically working on behalf of Anni, and on one occasion, about eight years into Anni's jail time, he told Anni that he and Erica were divorced, and Erica moved further up on the coast to the big city, and he has lost contact with her.

For the first time since Anni was in jail, tears filled her eyes, and she asked David why it had happened.

David was very reluctant to talk about it, but Anni kept prying.

"Well," David said, "Do you really want to know?"

Anni's short answer was, "Yes."

"Okay," David said, "I caught her cheating with one of my attorney colleagues in our own house."

This time, Anni did not ask any other questions. Just looking down on the jailhouse's visiting room floor, she shook her head up and down. Then she said to David: "How come you're still working on my behalf after all this?"

"Well," David said, "I respected you eight, nine years ago, and I respect you now even more. As a matter of fact, I've made an application on your behalf to the Governor of the State, for clemency."

"Oh, my God, David," said Anni, "Do you think there's a possibility that he might grant it to me? Or will I set myself up again with a false hope, like the past ten or twelve years?"

"No," said David. "I've reevaluated your whole case history with other attorneys, and they agree with me that you do."

Chapter XXV

On one glorious day, David stormed into Anni's prison cell.

"Anni, I have wonderful news for you. The Governor granted you a pardon. You'll be out of here in three days."

Anni just stood there looking at David. "You are not playing some cruel joke on me?" she asked.

"No, I would never do that," said David.

"I'll make all the arrangements, and I'll pick you up at your release."

Anni asked David, "What am I going to do? Where am I going to go? Nobody cares for me anymore."

David looked Anni straight in the eye, held her two delicate hands, and said, "Love never dies, and you're the proof of it. Your admirers abound, and I'm the living proof of that."

For the first time in ten years, Anni took a man's face in her hands, and gave a gentle kiss on David's cheek.

The third day, when Anni was to be released, she was up before dawn, and started to walk her cell's floor. She was very nervous, and a lot of contemplating bounced around in her head.

David came even earlier than the agreed time, and came into Anni's cell with the jail warden. The jail warden told Anni, in the presence of David, that the Governor of the State had pardoned her, and it was his greatest pleasure to inform Anni that she was free to go.

She was already dressed in the same outfit as she'd on ten years earlier, and David noticed that she has lost a little weight, but still looked beautiful.

They checked out of the jail, and David insisted to Anni that he had made all the arrangements to take Anni to the coast without stopping anywhere except at the airport.

Anni said, "All right, you are acting like you're my son.

"I feel like I'm your son," said David.

Anni kissed David's cheek and said, "I do love you like a mother would love her son."

Then David planted a soft kiss on Anni's cheek, and they left in the pre-arranged waiting limo for the airport.

Anni was at Haidy and David's house on the coast for six days, soaking in the warm sunshine and freedom.

David gave her all the financial documents, as Anni had sold her condo ten years earlier, and all the money was invested in Anni's name. Actually, Anni was better off financially now than ever before in her life.

She was told that all her clothes were taken care of, and all her things were in the one room in their house where nobody went, except to clean and refresh her garments. Her red sports car had been sold and the money was also invested with the rest. All her jewelry was put into a safe box by David, with Anni's name on it.

Anni felt awkward. These people took care of all her stuff and affairs perfectly, and she mentioned it to them.

David said laughingly, "Well, isn't that partially what you hired me as an attorney for? All I've done is the attorney's duty, and I'm sure any one of them would've performed the service to you just as good as I did."

"Sure," said Anni.

They all started laughing.

David took Anni car shopping, and Anni kept asking David which one he liked.

David said: "Anni, this is going to be your car, come on."

"No," Anni said, "I won't buy it unless you tell me that you could fall in love with my choice."

Then they went car shopping at the Mercedes Benz dealership, and David kept looking at the 560 Sports Model. Anni made believe she did not notice this, and said to David after looking at all the cars that she liked the Red 560 Sports Model.

She asked David, "What about it? Do you like my choice?"

"Who wouldn't?" was David's answer.

"I know," said Anni, "But do you?"

"Oh, I love it," said David.

Anni bought the car.

Anni had to wait two days before the new car was delivered, and spent the days chit-chatting during the daytime with Haidy, because David was busy back in his office.

After Anni's car was delivered, she asked David to take her for a ride in it for the first time, since he knew more about cars than she did.

David obliged, and even took the day off for it.

Anni was looking at David's face from the side, and as he got in the red Mercedes, his face lit up. All he did was tell Anni how good it handled, and how beautiful it was.

David didn't know that Anni was happier than David, for David.

When they returned to the villa, Anni asked David if he could find out Erica's present address, or at least phone number.

"Oh, I don't know," said David, "It's been a while, and nobody knows where she is."

"Okay, then," Anni said, "I'm hiring you on a retainer to find out, okay? Would you do that for me?" she asked.

He answered, "I can try, but I won't guarantee it."

"Okay," said Anni.

Days went by, and then weeks, and Anni told Haidy that maybe she should try to get her own place, but Haidy would not have it. She said: "You're now family and you stay with us."

Anni thanked her, but she knew that the arrangement, at least on her part, was temporary.

About four weeks after Anni gave the assignment to David, she approached him at the pool-side.

"David," she asked, "did you find Erica?"

"No, not yet," he said. "But looking."

Looking at his face, something told Anni that he was not telling her the complete truth.

A week later, she attempted the same question, and David told her, "Yes, but I'm not sure if I want to tell you."

"Why not?" she asked.

"Because Erica told me not to."

"Don't worry about it," Anni reassured David, "I won't tell her that you told me. I'll tell her that I found it out for myself."

He gave her Erica's address. "Look. Remember that I didn't want to give it to you."

Next day Anni was in her car coasting up north of the coast in the direction of the cosmopolitan city where Erica's address was. When she arrived at the address that David gave her, she said to herself, "No, this can't be it."

It was an old, gothic-looking, neglected house.

Well, she thought, let me knock on the door to make sure that I'm at the wrong address, and then I can call back David to straighten out the situation. She knocked at the broken entrance door of the building, and as the woman opened the door, Anni knew that she wouldn't have to call David back.

In front of her was her daughter, Erica, looking scrungy -- her hair all over the place, her dress was ripped in a few places, and she looked dirty and well beyond her real age. She held a burning cigarette in her hand, and her eyes looked like she had consumed ten straight Martinis in a row, just thirty minutes ago.

She said to Anni, "Hello. What the hell are you doing here?" she was as high as a kite.

Anni, said "I'm free. I was pardoned from the Governor, and I couldn't wait to see you."

"Well," Erica said, "You saw me, now you can go back."

Anni said, "Come on Erica, I haven't seen you in ten years. Can I please talk to you?"

"I don't want to talk to you," was Erica's reply.

"I'll tell you what," Anni, said, "you give me twenty minutes to talk to you, and I won't bother you after that, if you don't want me to. Is it a deal?"

Erica looked at Anni, and with cigarette in mouth, she waved to Anni, "All right, come on in, but no remarks on my place or anything else, or I'll throw you out."

Anni agreed and they went in.

Anni wished she had not asked Erica to invite her inside. The place looked like a Mack truck went through it -- rags were all over, the curtains were ripped and hanging half-on and half-off of the rods, she could not see the color of the floor for the dust and dirt, and the sunken, ripped sofa was where Erica told Anni to sit down.

Anni thought, Oh my God, I'll need a bath after I leave from here, and before I even can get into my car. But she was forced to get used to the odor and garbage for the duration of her conversation with Erica. She even noticed as she was sitting on the dirty couch, two cockroaches crawling up the wall.

"What's on your mind?" asked Erica.

"Well, first of all," said Anni, "I'd like to know what's happened to you in the past ten years."

"Why?" asked Erica.

"Because I care for you," replied Anni.

"Well," Erica said, "I got married, I got divorced, and now I'm a hooker. This is how I'm making my living."

"You call this living?" asked Anni.

"I told you, don't get smart on me."

Anni said, "Believe me honey, I'm not. But it hurts me to see you like this."

"It doesn't hurt me," said Erica, "I love it."

"Are you using drugs?" was the next inquiry from Anni.

"Amateur," answered Erica, "Can't you tell."

Of course, Anni could tell. She saw plenty of it in prison, but she was not going to confront Erica with her knowledge.

"And plenty of it, too, if I can afford it after five or six Johns a day," added Erica.

Anni knew it as soon as she opened the door that Erica looked used and abused, like a cheap five dollar whore that not even the dirtiest John wanted any more. "Please leave everything behind right now, and come away with me. I'll take care of you as long as I live. Let's start a new life together, and forget the past, as if it has never existed."

"All I have is the past," said Erica, "And no future. And now get out. I've had enough of this bullshit!"

Anni figured that she'd better leave and not press the issue. "Okay," Anni said, "I'm leaving." And then she got up and left.

As she got back into her car, she looked up to the sky, and said, "Oh Lord, why? Why are you taking everybody away from me?"

She headed for the next decent hotel, checked in, and figured she'd try again tomorrow to talk to Erica. Maybe she won't be high and Anni could reason with her.

The next day, when Anni went back to her daughter's place, Erica must have spotted her approach, because she came to the door and opened it before Anni was ten feet from it.

"What the hell are you doing here again?" was the substituted greeting from Erica.

Anni said, "I figured that today maybe you'd be in a better mood and be willing to talk to me."

Erica said, "I was in a better mood yesterday than today, and I never want to talk to you again."

This hurt Anni a lot more than yesterday, since she noticed that Erica wasn't high. "Okay," said Anni, "Give me a good reason why not, and I'll leave."

"I'll give you two reasons," was Erica's reply. "For this, you have to come in and sit down. Because once you've heard it, you're probably going to faint."

Anni went inside Erica's house and sat down on that same abused sofa. She was a little bit antsy to find out what was so devastating that Erica was going to tell her.

"Well," Erica opened up, "Do you remember the time when you came to the softball field, and told me that you were going to go out with Mr. Joe Cobb?"

"Yes, I do," said Anni.

"Remember that we were both laughing?"

"Yes, I do," said Anni.

"Well, let me tell you something," said Erica, "I was crying and dying inside."

"Why?" Anni asked.

"Because I was in love with Joe Cobb, and he had laid me four times previous to that occasion."

Anni was just sitting on this filthy sofa, like a concrete figure, listening to Erica's disgusting, but true, story.

"Secondly, when I found out that he was my father, you killed him. Do you want to know more?"

"No," Anni said, "That will do."

As Anni was getting up, Erica turned her around and said, "Don't ever come back into my life ever again. The day you killed Joe Cobb, you died."

Anni looked down at Erica's hand on her arm and said, "Take your hand off of me." With that, she left.

Anni went back to her hotel, laid down on the bed, and slowly tears came to her eyes, and her sobbing got louder, and culminated in something more resembling a rattle. She turned around and buried her face in the pillows. Anni didn't remember how long she was in this condition, because she fell asleep.

It was next day eight. She asked the concierge if he would know a place where they stored cars for at least a month for a fee. The concierge said yes, and gave Anni the number.

Anni went upstairs to her room, called the office of the garage, and the guy said he'd be there in a half an hour to pick up her car for storage. He came, and Anni paid him and got a contract copy from the storage company for her car.

Then she called the airline and got a noon reservation to fly back to her own State.

She ordered a taxi, and by ten she was sitting at the airport's coffee shop waiting for her flight. It was on time, and she boarded it.

But before she did, she made one more call to David. She informed him that everything was going to be all right, and that she would stay here in the city where Erica lived for one more week, and told him not to worry about anything.

"See you in six days or sooner," said Anni. "Thanks a million for everything you have done for me."

"No problem," was the remark from David, "See you in a week or before," and then they hung up.

Chapter XXVI

Anni arrived back in her State and called a lawyer.

He came right to her hotel room with two secretaries for witnesses, since Anni told him that she is making out her Last Will and Testament, and it had to be today, whatever the fee was for it.

That was all any attorney had to hear. He said, "Yes, ma'am, I'll be over within an hour," and he was with the two girls.

Then Anni called the cemetery where they buried Helen, asked for the plot number and ordered a complete overhaul of Helen's grave. She gave her credit card number and the guy asked her how soon she would like the job to be done. She answered, "Right away."

"Okay," the guy said, "I have plenty of time from early on tomorrow. It'll be done by ten o'clock."

Anni thanked him and called the florist. With the same credit card, she ordered a large amount of flowers to cover the entire grave of Helen.

The florist told Anni that the grave would be covered a foot high by eleven the next day.

The attorney, with the two girls, knocked on Anni's hotel door, ten minutes later.

Anni made out her Will, leaving everything to David Lang, with the exception of 10,000 dollars for Miss Slater.

She told the attorney where all her documents were at her other attorney's on the coast.

She paid the attorney, and he said he would stop in early the next morning at the coffee shop where Anni was staying to give her the copies of the Will.

He came next morning, right on time, and delivered the goods. They parted and Anni went upstairs in her room and called the cemetery to see if Helen's grave was ready.

"Oh, yes," the guy said. "It was done by nine-thirty." As a matter of fact, he informed Anni that the florist was there, and that Helen's grave looked like a flower garden piled up a foot high.

Anni thanked him and hung up. Then she took a shower, got dressed all in white, and with the hotel Bible, she went to visit Helen's grave. But before she left for the cemetery, she made one final phone call to an old-time connection. This guy sold her what she wanted for the right price -- a gun.

She arrived at Helen's grave at eleven. She looked over the grave, made a cross, and started to talk to Helen as if she were alive. Then she opened her Bible and read from it. She ended with the quotation, "That the God will give, and God will take it away."

She closed the Bible and laid it on Helen's headstone. Then she took out the gun from her pocket, and looking up into the sky, she said the following: "God, it's true that you shall give and you shall take it away. You have taken everybody away from me, but you missed me. So I am giving you a helping hand."

And with that, she laid down in the middle of the flowers that covered Helen's grave, raised the gun to her temple, and pulled the trigger.

At the sound of the gunshot, all the birds flew from the trees, and between them was only one white dove.

The cemetery groundskeeper was close enough to hear, and witness, Anni's suicide, but had only rushed over after he saw Anni laying down. He called the police.

Anni's blood discolored the white carnations to the color red around her head.

When the same detective who investigated Anni's previous cases arrived at the site, he did not disturb the scene. He yellow-taped around the grave, and called for the police department photographer. The police department photographer tipped off his buddies, the T.V. guys.

The waiting detective was eaten up inside, and wondered as he was looking at the scene, whether Anni's blood soaked through the soft ground, and maybe even was mingling with Helen's.

He knew that they were like sisters in life. He suspected that they are most likely in Heaven.

This detective also had a hobby of painting scenery, and as Anni's body was laying in the flowers on Helen's grave, he thought that if he would paint the picture, he would call it devotion.

As the newspapers the next day splashed the color pictures of the scene, the headlines above it said, "Heart-wrenching."

The police department's photographs were black and white, but the T.V.'s were in color. They were taken from a perfect angle, and the colors reminded one of a rainbow, late spring.

Chapter XXVII

David arranged for Anni's headstone, and it was an inlaid insertion of Jesus looking up to Heaven with praying hands. Anni's epitaph on the headstone read, "I wanted to live, and now I am a bride in Heaven."

David called Erica on the phone, but her phone was disconnected, and so he called one of his associate attorneys to check at Erica's house. The associate called David back the same day, and told him that according to the information he gathered from very good sources, Erica had stopped her shady business and moved in with the nuns at the remote hillside cloister.

David went to visit her. He wanted to tell Erica about her mother's death.

When the nuns let David in, and they brought Erica out in an outfit that was the beginning nun's uniform, David told her the sad story.

Erica made the sign of the cross on herself, and said, "God rest her soul."

David asked Erica why this enormous change in her life.

Erica answered, "At one time, we fell in love, and later we fell apart. Now I feel whole again, and in love with the Lord."

David was taken aback by Erica's regressed mark, and said: "God be with you, and soften the path that you'll walk on the rest of your life." Then he said goodbye and left.

David made all the necessary arrangements with the police

and the funeral home, including the flower shop and invitations to the funeral. He called Anni's local newspaper and put a large announcement in it.

David and Haidy arrived a day ahead of time before the viewing of Anni's remains. They checked into a nice hotel and confirmed with all the aforementioned professionals.

David had to do everything, since he could only find Erica, Anni's closest relative, a couple of days after Anni's death.

The first day at the funeral parlor, a lot of people showed up, except Erica. David and Haidy greeted all who came to show their respect, including Anni's former boss and colleagues, the D.A., Miss Slater, the Judge who presided on Anni's two trials, two famous T.V. anchormen, Helen's beauty parlor personnel, the ex-classmates of Erica, including the softball team, most of the local police department, with the two detectives, the lady coroner, Anni's neighbors from the condo, and others.

But there was nobody there from Anni's family, since Anni was an only child, and her parents had passed away years back, and they had no brothers and sisters.

Most of the funeral proceedings were discreetly televised.

As the investigating detective sat in a chair, paying his respects to Anni, the following came to his mind. How this case changed so many lives, but one thing had not changed: our law. He wondered who is eligible to decide things.

The big room at the funeral home where Anni was laid out, reminded one of a small sovereign nation, with Anni presiding.

Anni was prepared to perfection. She almost looked alive. The purity was radiating from her face, even now.

Anni seemed to be saying from her coffin, to all the women, "Don't forget what happened to me! If you forget it, then you will forget it at your peril. No woman, or child, is immune."

David's inside was shaking. As a final tribute to Anni; in front of the by now totally filled room, he walked over to her coffin. He knelt down and said a prayer, and maybe even something more in his silent conversation.

Then he got up, gently leaned over Anni's corpse, and gave a long kiss on her face.

Anni's face was almost saying: You have loved me.

The scene was almost invasive on the crowd's mind, and prompted some of the people's perverted mind to question, even now, if David was Anni's latest lover.

David noticed, and thought to himself, that some people never change. They don't have a virgin, but a diseased mind, and can't accept a pure, emotional love, and keep on hurting innocent and decent human beings.

The last day of the viewing of Anni's Thompson's remains, was standing room only in the funeral home. There were so many flowers sent that the funeral director was forced to push them closer to the wall, to give more room for the large crowd.

David walked up to the front microphone, and started to read his eulogy to the silent, huge crowd. The late afternoon sun was peeking in and out from behind the clouds; through the blinds of the room. David thought it was maybe jealous of Anni.

This fairly young, but sophisticated, gentleman, David Lang, could hardly contain himself, and as he said the first word of the eulogy -- "Anni" -- the tears broke out from his eyes, and he had to stop for a few seconds to dry them.

All the eyes of the softball team were filled with tears.

They knew that this was not softball. Here they could hit on something they could not see -- feelings.

David continued with his eulogy: "Dear Anni, ever since Adam and Eve were created, we have broken all the rules that God imposed on us. But the rule that we have broken against you, by blowing out the flame in your heart, that was pumping for the benefit of all human kind, will weigh very heavily on humanity for a long time to come.

"You were a lady."

"Up to your first trial, everybody thought the world of you. We have presided over you on two trials. Now, you are presiding over all of us as Judge, jury, and executioner. Please be kind and merciful in your judgment, and try to forgive our sin that we have committed against you. We will never forget you and all the goodness and decency that you have stood for. I have, and I do, love you."

With that, he stepped away from the microphone.

After this, nobody took the risk to utter one single word.

The priest led the crowd into a prayer, and then they disbursed.

The next morning, the church service was performed, and half of the city's police department was employed to organize the huge procession that left from the church to the cemetery where Anni was to be buried.

It was a cloudy day. It never rained, but was thundering, as to put in a final objection against lowering Anni's coffin into the hole.

Her coffin was lowered. Then, only one more loud thunder came.

The caretakers shovelled to cover the coffin, and piled to a two foot high heap. The flowers were piled on this, high and wide. The crowd disbursed, with the exception of one.

About twenty graves away from the crowd was standing a woman dressed completely in black, with a wide rimmed black hat and huge black sunglasses covering her eyes. She held a single red rose in her hand.

After the crowd left, she walked over to Anni's freshly covered grave. She removed her sunglasses. She was beautiful.

She said a prayer, and gently laid the single rose on top of the flowers. She looked up to Heaven, and in a loud sentence, said: "Mommy, I have loved you." Then she left to return to her hotel room, where she changed back into her nun's uniform, and returned to the cloister.

After leaving Anni's funeral, for some unexplainable reason, I started to walk toward the same coffee shop where Anni and Joe had their first date. I sat down at the same table as they did.

I ordered for myself a stiff Martini, and silently made the following statement: I am definitely against killing and suicide.

But wherever Anni went, Heaven or Hell, it was a better place for Anni than here on earth.

I could not sustain my inner frustration, and my soul could have used a little cuddling.

As I was saying this to myself, two tears ran down my cheeks. As they dropped to the table, I raised my head towards the Heavens, and said, "They are for you, Anni."

End

Afterword

I have followed the Anni Thompson story from the beginning to the end.

The diary that Anni wrote in her ten years of prison duration was a great help to me writing this book. Therefore, I will be forever indebted to Anni Thompson.

No other history from a woman ever affected me personally as much as Anni's.

This was what compelled me to tell it for the world.

Zoltan Karpathy

"About the Writer"

Zoltan Karpathy is a world traveler, speaking four languages, and a firm believer that life is a classroom, where experience and knowledge is inexhaustible.

Zoltan was involved in the entertainment business, and the ex-owner of three restaurants and clubs. He is an accomplished writer of several other books to be published in the very near future.

9 781587 210679